I CROSSED MY ARMS. There was no way she was getting our money. "That money's for Disneyland," I told her.

"To go on all the rides."

"And meet Tinker Bell."

This was the first time we heard Cecile laugh, and she laughed like the crazy mother she was turning out to be. "Is Tinker Bell going to feed you?" She was still laughing.

ONe CRazy SummeR

by Rita Williams-Garcia

Amistad
An Imprint of HarperCollinsPublishers

Amistad is an imprint of HarperCollins Publishers.

One Crazy Summer
Copyright © 2010 by Rita Williams-Garcia
All rights reserved. Printed in the United States of America.
No part of this book may be used or reproduced in any manner whatsoever
without written permission except in the case of brief quotations embodied
in critical articles and reviews. For information address HarperCollins
Children's Books, a division of HarperCollins Publishers, 195 Broadway,
New York, NY 10007.
www.harpercollinschildrens.com

Library of Congress Cataloging-in-Publication Data
Williams-Garcia, Rita.
    One crazy summer / Rita Williams-Garcia. — 1st ed.
        p.   cm.
    Summary: In the summer of 1968, after traveling from Brooklyn
to Oakland, California, to spend a month with the mother they barely
know, eleven-year-old Delphine and her two younger sisters arrive to a
cold welcome as they discover that their mother, a dedicated poet and
printer, is resentful of the intrusion of their visit and wants them to
attend a nearby Black Panther summer camp.
    ISBN 978-0-06-076090-8
    [1.   Sisters—Fiction. 2.   Mothers—Fiction. 3.   Poets—Fiction.
4.   African   Americans—Fiction. 5.   Black   Panther   Party—Fiction.
6. Civil rights movements—Fiction. 7. Oakland (Calif.)—History—20th
century—Fiction.] I. Title.
PZ7.W6713On   2010   2009009293
[Fic]—dc22   CIP
                                                                          AC

Typography by Ola Kapusto
17 18 19 20 CG/OPM 32

First paperback edition, 2012

For the late Churne Lloyd,
and especially for
Maryhana, Kamau, Ife, and Oni

Cassius Clay Clouds

Good thing the plane had seat belts and we'd been strapped in tight before takeoff. Without them, that last jolt would have been enough to throw Vonetta into orbit and Fern across the aisle. Still, I anchored myself and my sisters best as I could to brace us for whatever came next. Those clouds weren't through with us yet and dealt another Cassius Clay–left–and–a–right jab to the body of our Boeing 727.

Vonetta shrieked, then stuck her thumb in her mouth. Fern bit down on Miss Patty Cake's pink plastic arm. I kept my whimper to myself. It was bad enough my insides squeezed in and stretched out like a monkey grinder's accordion—no need to let anyone know how frightened I was.

I took a breath so, when my mouth finally opened, I'd sound like myself and not like some scared rabbit. "It's just the clouds bumping," I told my sisters. "Like they bumped over Detroit and Chicago and Denver."

Vonetta pulled her thumb out of her mouth and put her head in her lap. Fern held on to Miss Patty Cake. They listened to me.

"We push our way up in the clouds; the clouds get mad and push back. Like you and Fern fighting over red and gold crayons." I didn't know about clouds fighting and pushing for a fact, but I had to tell my sisters something. As long as Vonetta kept her fear to one shriek and Fern kept hers to biting Miss Patty Cake, I kept on spinning straw, making everything all right. That's mainly what I do. Keep Vonetta and Fern in line. The last thing Pa and Big Ma wanted to hear was how we made a grand Negro spectacle of ourselves thirty thousand feet up in the air around all these white people.

"You know how Papa is," I told them. "No way he'd put us on a plane if it were dangerous."

They halfway believed me. Just as I had that soft plastic arm out of Fern's mouth, those Cassius Clay–fighting clouds threw our 727 another jab.

Big Ma—that's Pa's mother—still says Cassius Clay. Pa says Muhammad Ali or just Ali. I slide back and forth from Cassius Clay to Muhammad Ali. Whatever picture comes to mind. With Cassius Clay you hear the clash of fists, like the plane getting jabbed and punched. With Muhammad Ali you see a mighty mountain, greater than Everest, and can't no one knock down a mountain.

All the way to the airport, Pa had tried to act like he was dropping off three sacks of wash at the Laundromat. I'd seen through Pa. He's no Vonetta, putting on performances. He has only one or two faces, nothing hidden, nothing exaggerated. Even though it had been his idea that we fly out to Oakland to see Cecile, Pa'd never once said how exciting our trip would be. He just said that seeing Cecile was something whose time had come. That it had to be done. Just because he decided it was time for us to see her didn't mean he wanted us to go.

My sisters and I had stayed up practically all night California dreaming about what seemed like the other side of the world. We saw ourselves riding wild waves on surfboards, picking oranges and apples off fruit trees, filling our autograph books with signatures from movie stars we'd see in soda shops. Even better, we saw ourselves going to Disneyland.

We had watched airplanes lift up and fly off into blue sky as we neared the airport. Every time another airliner flew overhead, leaving a trail of white and gray smoke, Big Ma fanned herself and asked, "Jesus, why?"

Big Ma had kept quiet long enough. Once inside the terminal, she let it all hang out. She told Pa, "I don't mind saying it, but this isn't right. Coming out to Idlewild and

3

putting these girls on a plane so Cecile can see what she left behind. If she wants to see, let her get on an airplane and fly out to New York."

Big Ma doesn't care if President Kennedy's face is on the half-dollar or if the airport is now officially named after him. She calls the airport by its old name, Idlewild. Don't get me wrong. Big Ma was as mad and sad as anyone when they killed the president. It's change she has no pity on. However things are stamped in Big Ma's mind is how they will be, now and forever. Idlewild will never be JFK. Cassius Clay will never be Muhammad Ali. Cecile will never be anything other than Cecile.

I can't say I blamed Big Ma for feeling the way she did. I certainly didn't forgive Cecile.

When Cecile left, Fern wasn't on the bottle. Vonetta could walk but wanted to be picked up. I was four going on five. Pa wasn't sick, but he wasn't doing well, either. That was when Big Ma came up from Alabama to see about us.

Even though Big Ma read her Scripture daily, she hadn't considered forgiveness where Cecile was concerned. Cecile wasn't what the Bible meant when it spoke of love and forgiveness. Only judgment, and believe me, Big Ma had plenty of judgment for Cecile. So even if Cecile showed up on Papa's welcome mat, Big Ma wouldn't swing the front door open.

That was why Pa had put us on a plane to Oakland.

Either Cecile wouldn't come back to Brooklyn or she wasn't welcome. Honestly, I don't think Pa could choose between Big Ma and Cecile even after Cecile left him. And us. Even after Cecile proved Big Ma right.

"How can you send them to Oakland? Oakland's nothing but a boiling pot of trouble cooking. All them riots."

Pa has a respectful way of ignoring Big Ma. I wanted to smile. He's good at it.

A shrill voice had announced the departing flight to Oakland. All three of us had butterflies. Our first airplane ride. Way up above Brooklyn. Above New York. Above the world! Although I could at least keep still, Vonetta and Fern stamped their feet like holy rollers at a revival meeting.

Big Ma had grabbed them by the first scruff of fabric she could get ahold of, bent down, and told them to "act right." There weren't too many of "us" in the waiting area, and too many of "them" were staring.

I'd taken a quick count out of habit. Vonetta, Fern, and I were the only Negro children. There were two soldier boys in green uniforms who didn't look any older than Uncle Darnell—high school cap and gown one day, army boots and basic training four days later. Two teenage girls with Afros. Maybe they were college students. And one lady dressed like Jackie Kennedy, carrying a small oval suitcase.

Big Ma had also scouted around the waiting room. I

knew she worried that we'd be mistreated in some way and sought out a grown, brown face to look out for us. Big Ma turned her nose up at the college girls with Afros in favor of the Negro lady in the square sunglasses and snappy suit toting the equally snappy oval bag. Big Ma made eye contact with her. When we lined up, she'd told the Negro Jackie Kennedy, "These my grandbabies. You look out for them, y'hear." The snappy Negro lady had been nice enough to smile but hadn't returned the look that Big Ma expected—and Big Ma had expected the look Negro people silently pass each other. She'd expected this stranger to say, as if she were a neighbor, "They're as good as my own. I'll make sure they don't misbehave or be an embarrassment to the Negro race." A blank movie-star smile had been all she passed to Big Ma. That lady had only been looking out for her plane seat.

Papa had already given me a paper with the phone number to our house, which I knew by heart, and the phone number to his job. He had already told me that his job number was for emergencies only and not for "how you doing" chats. Last night he had also given me an envelope with two hundred dollars in ten- and twenty-dollar bills to put in my suitcase. Instead, I'd folded the bills and stuffed them in my tennis shoe before we left Herkimer Street. Walking on that mound of money felt weird at first, but at least I knew the money was safe.

Papa had kissed Vonetta and Fern and told me to look

after my sisters. Even though looking after them would have been nothing new, I kissed him and said, "I will, Papa."

When the line to the ticket taker had begun to move, Big Ma had gotten teary and mushed us up in her loose-fitting, violet and green muumuu dress. "Better come on and get some loving now . . ." She hadn't had to finish the rest about how this might be the last time in a long while for kissing and hugging. A flash of memory told me Cecile wasn't one for kissing and hugging.

I had a lot of those memories clicking before me like projector slides in the dark. Lots of pictures, smells, and sounds flashing in and out. Mostly about Cecile, all going way, way back. And what I didn't remember clearly, Uncle Darnell always filled in. At least Uncle Darnell remembers Cecile kindly.

Golden Gate Bridge

I glanced at my Timex. Among the three of us, I was the only one responsible enough to keep and wear a wristwatch. Vonetta let a girl "see hers" and never got it back. Fern was still learning to tell time, so I kept hers in my drawer until she was ready to wear it.

Six and a half hours had passed since we'd hugged Big Ma and kissed Pa at John F. Kennedy Airport. The clouds had made peace with our Boeing 727. It was safe to breathe. I stretched as far as my legs could go.

With these long legs I'm taken for twelve or thirteen, even a little older. No one ever guesses eleven going on twelve on their first try. More than my long legs, I'm sure it's my plain face that throws them off. Not plain as in homely plain, but *even* plain. Steady. I'm not nine or seven and given to squealing or oohing like Vonetta and Fern. I just let my plain face and plain words speak for me. That way, no one ever says, "Huh?" to me. They know exactly what I mean.

We were long gone from thick, white clouds, the plane steadily climbing down. The intercom crackled, and the pilot made an announcement about the descent and altitude and that we would be landing in ten minutes. I let all of that pass by until he said, ". . . and to your left as we circle the bay is the Golden Gate Bridge."

I was now a liar! A stone-faced liar. I wanted to squeal and ooh like a seven-year-old meeting Tinker Bell. I had read about the Golden Gate Bridge in class. The California gold rush. The Chinese immigrants building the railroads connecting east to west. It wasn't every day you saw a live picture of what you read about in your textbook. I wanted to look down from above the world and see the Golden Gate Bridge.

Being stuck in the middle seat, I was mad at myself. Of the three of us, I was the first to board the 727. Why hadn't I taken the window seat when I'd had my chance?

Instead of the squeal I knew wouldn't come out of me in the first place, I sighed. No use crying about it now. The truth was, one pout from either Vonetta or Fern and I would have given up the window seat.

This was the only way it could be: Vonetta and Fern on

either side and me in between them. Six and a half hours was too long a time to have Vonetta and Fern strapped side by side picking at each other. We would have been the grand Negro spectacle that Big Ma had scolded us against becoming when we were back in Brooklyn.

Still, the Golden Gate Bridge was getting away from me. I figured at least one of us should see it. And that should be the one who read about it in class.

"Look, Vonetta. Look down at the bridge!"

Vonetta stayed tight to her stubborn curl, her chin in her lap. "I'm not looking."

I turned to my right and got a mouthful of hair and barrettes. Fern had leaned over from her aisle seat. "I wanna see. Make her switch." To Fern, the Golden Gate Bridge sounded like Sleeping Beauty's castle. She halfway believed in things not true and didn't know where fairy tales ended. No use spoiling it for her. She'd figure things out soon enough.

Fern was wriggling out of her seat belt and climbing on me to get a glimpse. This was how it was at home. Why should a thousand feet up in the air make any difference? "Sit back, Fern," I said in my plain, firm voice. "We're getting ready to land."

She pouted but sat back down. I tightened her seat belt. Vonetta's face stayed in her lap. That was just pitiful.

"Go look down, Vonetta," I said. "Before you miss it."

Vonetta refused to pry her chin from her lap. She stuck

her thumb back in her mouth and closed her eyes.

I wasn't worried about Vonetta. Once we got on the ground, she'd be her showy self again and this fraidycat episode would be long faded.

As we continued to circle the bay above the Golden Gate Bridge, I felt like I was being teased for the simple act of wanting. Each time the plane curved around I knew in my heart it would be my last chance and the bridge was singing, "Na-na-na-na-na. You can't see me."

Now, I had to see the bridge. How many times would I be this high up and have a sight as spectacular as the Golden Gate Bridge right underneath me? I loosened my seat belt, lifted myself, and leaned over Vonetta's head and shoulders to get a look out of the oval window. I pressed against Vonetta. Just a little. Not enough to cause a stir. But Vonetta and Fern, who was now angry, both hollered, "Delphine!" as loud as they could.

Heads turned our way. A stewardess rushed to our row. "Sit in your seat, missy," she scolded me. "We're getting ready to land."

Even though there were only eight Negroes on board, counting my sisters and me, I had managed to disgrace the entire Negro race, judging by the head shaking and *tsk-tsk*ing going on around us. I shifted my behind into my seat and tightened my seat belt. But not before I had seen orange steel poking through thick ground clouds below. Smog.

There was no time to savor my victory or feel my shame. The plane went roaring down farther and farther. Vonetta held on to my left arm, and Fern, with Miss Patty Cake, grabbed my right. I dug into the armrests and prayed the pilot had done this before.

The plane bounced off the ground as soon as we hit land. It kept bouncing and surging forward until the bouncing smoothed out and we were rolling against the ground, nice and steady.

I took a deep breath so I'd sound like myself when I started telling Vonetta and Fern what to do. The main thing was we were on the ground. We were in Oakland.

Secret Agent Mother

The Negro lady with the snappy oval bag didn't give us a glance as she *click-clack*ed on by. That was fine with me, although I'd tell Big Ma otherwise if she asked, just to keep her from worrying. And I'd make it short and simple. I only get caught if I try to spin too much straw.

With both feet safely on the ground, Vonetta became her old self, her face shiny and searching. "What do we call her?"

I'd gone over this with Vonetta and Fern many, many times. I told them long before Papa said we were going to meet her. I told them while we packed our suitcases. "Her name is Cecile. That's what you call her. When people ask who she is, you say, 'She is our mother.'"

Mother is a statement of fact. Cecile Johnson gave birth to us. We came out of Cecile Johnson. In the animal kingdom that makes her our mother. Every mammal on the planet has a mother, dead or alive. Ran off or stayed put. Cecile Johnson—mammal birth giver, alive, an abandoner—is our mother. A statement of fact.

Even in the song we sing when we miss having a mother—and not her but a mother, period—we sing about a mother. "Mother's gotta go now, la-la-la-la-la . . ." Never Mommy, Mom, Mama, or Ma.

Mommy gets up to give you a glass of water in the middle of the night. Mom invites your friends inside when it's raining. Mama burns your ears with the hot comb to make your hair look pretty for class picture day. Ma is sore and worn out from wringing your wet clothes and hanging them to dry; Ma needs peace and quiet at the end of the day.

We don't have one of those. We have a statement of fact.

Vonetta, Fern, and I stood next to the young redheaded stewardess assigned to watch us until Cecile came forward. The stewardess reread the slip of paper in her hand, then eyed the big clock mounted by the arrival-and-departure board, as if she had someplace else to be. She could have left me alone with my sisters. I certainly didn't need her.

A man in navy overalls swept garbage off the floor a few feet away from us. He went about his job with no expression, sweeping cigarette packs and gum wrappers into a dustpan that he emptied into a larger trash can. If I were him, picking up after people who carelessly dropped stuff on the ground, I'd be nothing but angry.

They call it littering when you carelessly drop things. They call the careless folks who drop things by a cute name: litterbug.

There's nothing cute about dropping things carelessly. Dropping garbage and having puppies shouldn't be called the same thing. "Litter." I had a mind to write to Miss Webster about that. Puppies don't deserve to be called a litter like they had been dropped carelessly like garbage. And people who litter shouldn't be given a cute name for what they do. And at least the mother of a litter sticks around and nurses her pups no matter how sharp their teeth are. Merriam Webster was falling down on the job. How could she have gotten this wrong?

Vonetta asked me again. Not because she was anxious to meet Cecile. Vonetta asked again so she could have her routine rehearsed in her head—her curtsy, smile, and greeting—leaving Fern and me to stand around like dumb dodos. She was practicing her role as the cute, bouncy pup in the litter and asked yet again, "Delphine, what do we call her?"

A large white woman came and stood before us, clapping her hands like we were on display at the Bronx Zoo. "Oh, my. What adorable dolls you are. My, my." She warbled like an opera singer. Her face was moon full and jelly soft, the cheeks and jaw framed by white whiskers.

We said nothing.

"And so well behaved."

Vonetta perked up to out-pretty and out-behave us.

I did as Big Ma had told me in our many talks on how to act around white people. I said, "Thank you," but I didn't add the "ma'am," for the whole "Thank you, ma'am." I'd never heard anyone else say it in Brooklyn. Only in old movies on TV. And when we drove down to Alabama. People say "Yes, ma'am," and "No, ma'am" in Alabama all the time. That old word was perfectly fine for Big Ma. It just wasn't perfectly fine for me.

The lady opened her pocketbook, took out a red leather change purse, and scooted coins around, searching for the right amount for adorable, well-behaved colored dolls. Big Ma would have thought that was grand, but Papa wouldn't have liked it one cent. Now it was time to do what Papa had told me: see after my sisters.

"We're not allowed to take money from strangers." I said this polite enough to suit Big Ma but strong enough to suit Papa.

The redheaded stewardess was appalled by my uppity behavior. "Don't you know when someone is being nice to you?"

I put on my dumb dodo face to fake not knowing what she meant.

What was the sense of making the stewardess stand guard over us if she refused to protect us from strangers? She thought it was all right to have the large white woman gawk at us, talk to us, and buy our attention. We might as well have stood by ourselves.

I didn't have to shift my eyes to see mile-long pouts on Vonetta and Fern. I didn't care. We weren't taking nothing from no strangers.

The lady was all smiles and squeals. Her face shook with laughter. "Oh, and so cute." She put all the nickels in Fern's hand and pinched her cheek faster than I could do anything about it and was gone, as big as she was.

Vonetta grabbed Fern's hand, forced it open, and took her nickel, leaving our two coins in Fern's palm. No use telling them to hand the money over. They were already dreaming of penny candy. I let them keep their nickels and mine.

The stewardess reexamined the slip of paper. She shifted from one leg to the other. Both my sisters and me, and her high heels, were bothering her.

I looked around the crowd of people pacing and waiting. Papa didn't keep any pictures of Cecile, but I had a sense of her. Fuzzy flashes of her always came and went. But I knew she was big, as in tall, and Hershey colored like me. I knew I at least had that right.

Then something made me look over to my left at a figure

standing by the cigarette machine. She moved, then moved back, maybe deciding whether to come to us or not. I told the stewardess before the figure could slip out of the airport, "That's her."

Fern and Vonetta were excited and scared. They squeezed my hands tight. I could see any thoughts Vonetta had about reciting poetry, tap-dancing, and curtsying vanished. She squeezed my hand harder than Fern did.

The stewardess marched us on over to this figure. Once we were there, face-to-face, the stewardess stopped in her tracks and made herself a barrier between the strange woman and us. The same stewardess who let the large white woman gawk at us and press money into Fern's hand wasn't so quick to hand us over to the woman I said was our mother. I wanted to be mad, but I couldn't say I blamed her entirely. It could have been the way the woman was dressed. Big black shades. Scarf tied around her head. Over the scarf, a big hat tilted down, the kind Pa wore with a suit. A pair of man's pants.

Fern clung to me. Cecile looked more like a secret agent than a mother. But I knew she was Cecile. I knew she was our mother.

"Are you . . ."—the stewardess unfurled the crumpled slip of paper—"Cecile Johnson?" She paused heavily between the first and last names. "Are you these colored girls' momma?"

Cecile looked at us, then at the stewardess. "I'm Cecile

Johnson. These"—she motioned to us—"are mine."

That was all the stewardess needed to hear. She dropped the slip of paper on the floor, handed us over, and fled away on her wobbly high heels.

Cecile didn't bother to grab any of our bags. She said, "Come on," took two wide steps, and we came. The gap between Cecile and us spread wider and wider. Vonetta sped up but was annoyed that she had to. Fern could only go so fast with her bag in one hand and Miss Patty Cake in the other. And I wasn't going anywhere without Vonetta or Fern, so I slowed down.

Cecile finally turned as she got to the glass doors and looked to see where we were. When we caught up, she said, "Y'all have to move if you're going to be with me."

"Fern needs help," I told her. Then Fern said, "I do not," and Vonetta said, "I need help."

Cecile's face had no expression. She swooped down, grabbed Fern's bag handle, and said, "Y'all keep up." She started walking, the same wide steps as before.

I took Fern's hand and we all followed. The gap wasn't as wide as when we'd first started out, but there was distance between Cecile and my sisters and me. Mobs easily threaded through and around us. You couldn't see we were together.

There was something uncommon about Cecile. Eyes glommed onto her. Tall, dark brown woman in man's pants whose face was half hidden by a scarf, hat, and big dark shades. She was like a colored movie star. Tall, mysterious, and on the run. Mata Hari in the airport. Except there weren't any cameras or spies following the colored, broad-shouldered Mata Hari. Only three girls trailing her from a slight distance.

We followed her outside, where green and white cabs lined up. Instead of going to the first cab in the line, Cecile ducked her head and searched every other cab. It was at the fourth cab that she bent down and rapped against the window. The driver, wearing a black beret, leaned over, nodded, unlocked the front door, and said something like "Zilla," which I guessed was short for Cecile in a colored, Oakland way.

Cecile opened the back door. "Come on."

I asked, "Can we put our bags in the—"

"Girl, will you get in this car?"

Vonetta and Fern stiffened. Big Ma could be hard. Papa didn't play around. But no one talked to me like that. It was just as Big Ma had said. We were in a boiling pot of trouble cooking. Still, there was no time to soothe my pride. I had to make everything all right for Vonetta and Fern so they'd fall in line. I got in first with my bag, pulling Fern in with me while she held on to Miss Patty Cake, and then Vonetta got in with her bag.

Cecile and the cab driver lit up cigarettes as we drove on. At least Papa doesn't smoke his Viceroys in the Wildcat. Vonetta coughed, and Fern looked green. I didn't bother to ask what I could and could not do. I cranked down my window to let the air in.

We were quiet. Riding along. Gazing out the windows at Oakland and stealing looks at Cecile. Before I could get a thought going about Cecile or Oakland, the cab driver let us out not too far from the airport.

"You live near the airport?" Vonetta asked.

Cecile didn't answer. She just said, "Come on."

As we walked, she hid deeper into her hat and shades, like she didn't want anyone to see her with us.

Was she ashamed she had three girls she'd left behind and had to explain? *Who are these girls? Yours? Why don't they live with you?*

Don't expect no pity from us. We were asked the same questions in Brooklyn. *Where's your mother? Why don't she live with you? Is it true she died?*

Cecile placed Fern's suitcase on the bench of a bus stop and sat down.

"Why are we taking the bus?" Vonetta asked. "Why didn't the cab take us?"

I shushed Vonetta just to keep Cecile from saying something mean.

By my Timex, the bus came in four minutes. Cecile made us get on first and said, "Go all the way to the back and sit down." When we found seats, Cecile was still with the bus driver, arguing with him. "Ten and under ride for free," she said. "Now give me four transfers."

I had been eleven for a good while, standing tall; but I said to Vonetta and Fern, "If anyone asks, I'm ten."

Vonetta folded her arms. "Well, I'm still nine. I am not going back to eight."

Fern said, "I'm staying seven."

I hushed them both down. A lotta good it did if the bus driver heard us getting our ages straight. Tell the truth, it was Cecile I worried about, not the driver. We didn't have to stay with the bus driver for the next twenty-eight days. We had to stay with Cecile.

Green Stucco House

Big Ma said Cecile lived on the street. The park bench was her bed. She lived in a hole in the wall.

You can't say stuff like that to a kid asking about her mother when it's snowing outside or pouring down raining. You can't say, "Your mother lives on the street, in a hole in the wall, sleeping on park benches next to winos."

I didn't understand expressions when I was six. That they were strings of words spoken so often, the string fell slack. "Your mother lives on the street, in a hole in the wall, sleeping on park benches next to winos" sounded exactly as Big Ma said it. When you're six, you picture your mother living on black and gray tar full of potholes, broken glass, skid marks, and blackened gum, all of that overrun by cars, buses, and trucks. You squeeze your brain one way, your imagination the other way, and see your mother peeking out the holes of crumbling abandoned buildings to stay dry when it snowed or rained. You see your mother sleeping on splintery park benches stained with pigeon poop and a smelly, toothless wino sleeping next to her. When you're six, you wonder why your mother would rather live on the street, in a hole in the wall, and sleep on park benches next to winos than live with you.

Even though I'd finally figured out these were expressions and not the plain, factual truth, I expected Cecile Johnson to, at the very least, be bad off. To be one of those "Negroes living in poverty," as the news often put it. I expected I'd have to nudge Vonetta and Fern into knowing better when they asked for all the things we had at home, like Mr. Bubble bubble bath, extra helpings of chicken and ham, or banana pudding on Sundays.

When Cecile slowed her man-sized steps, tore off her big hat, her scarf, and her dark glasses, we knew we had arrived. We followed her into the yard and down the walkway. I stared at her eight thick braids of unpressed hair, pencils shoved in the plait above her ear. Then I joined my sisters, taking in the shock of her house and yard. The place where she lived.

"This your house?" Vonetta was the first to put our amazement into words.

To begin with, the house was covered in peaks of

hard green frosting. Stucco, Cecile called it. She said she applied the stucco herself. The green prickly house was surrounded by a dried-out but neatly trimmed lawn. To one side of the house was a rectangular concrete slab with a roof over it. A carport, she said. Just no car. On the other side, a baby palm tree sloped toward the sun. That palm tree was as out of place as the stucco. That's how I could be sure it was Cecile's home, all right.

Even though Cecile said the house was hers and not to worry about how she got it, that wasn't enough to suit Vonetta.

"Big Ma said—"

I kicked her before she could go further. She knew better than to repeat Big Ma's words; and if she didn't, that kick should have smarted her into knowing better.

Whether Cecile heard Vonetta starting to insult her or if she saw me kick her second child, she didn't let on. She just said, "Come on," and put the key in the door.

We walked inside and looked around. I expected to see writing on the walls. Wavy, colored hippie writing all over, since she was free to do what she wanted in her own house. I expected to read strings and strings of words tapped out from her pencil onto the walls. But the walls in Cecile's house were clean, painted a yellow beige, and had no writing. Still, flashes of memory popped before me. Flashes of Cecile writing on the walls, and on boxes . . . Flashes of paint smells . . . Papa painting over her pencil marks . . .

Flashes of loud . . . Papa and Cecile. Angry talking. When I'd asked about it, Uncle Darnell had said they'd fought over Cecile writing on the walls all the time.

"Your room's in the back. Bathroom across the hall. The daybed rolls out. That should be enough for all y'all."

Fern folded her arms, holding Miss Patty Cake by a tuft of her patchy, yellow hair. "We need night-beds. We sleep at night."

I could tell Cecile didn't know whether to be annoyed or amused. She looked at all of us wondering not only who we were, but *what* we were.

Fern didn't notice the scrutiny. She turned to me. "I don't nap in the daytime. I'm in the second grade."

Never to be outdone, Vonetta said, "I'm in the fourth grade."

Cecile said, "I didn't ask for all that."

As I expected, Vonetta's feelings got hurt because she was always sticking herself onstage for everyone to see her. Still, Vonetta hadn't been kicked enough. She whirled around in the living room like a dance-recital fairy. Whirled around on her heels—taking in the clean walls, the curtains, a beat-up sofa, a few stacks of books, and not much else—landed, and said, "Where's the TV and everything?"

Vonetta was too far from me to nudge or kick.

Cecile dropped Fern's bag on the floor and started muttering, "I didn't send for you. Didn't want you in the first place. Should have gone to Mexico to get rid of you when I had the chance."

It didn't seem like she was talking to us. She didn't even look at Vonetta. Or Fern and me. She kept talking, muttering about Mexico, throwing her Mata Hari disguise on the beat-up sofa.

Our mother wore pencils in her hair, dressed like a secret agent, had a stickly, prickly house, a palm tree when no one else had one, and clean, painted walls instead of the writing I remembered. Now I got why our mother ran away. Our mother was crazy.

"Come on," I said. "Let's see the room. Put our stuff away."

Vonetta and Fern raced down the hall, pushing to be first. Cecile yelled after them, but they were too excited to hear her.

I came in after them. A bed with a brass headboard and arm rails, a blue cover. A dresser. A goosenecked floor lamp with a glass bowl in the shape of a half-moon. It was more furniture than she had in the living room.

"We can't all fit on this one bed," Vonetta said.

I raised up the blue cover and found the other bed underneath.

"Come on. Help me pull it out."

We all latched on and pulled. The bed rolled out into a stair step of one bed below and another above.

I said, "She should have helped us."

"Surely should have," Fern said.

"I sleep on top," Vonetta called.

"No, I sleep on top."

Fern did her best Rocky the Flying Squirrel leap, arms outstretched to belly onto the bed. Vonetta followed, and they wrapped into wrestling. I let them. They hadn't had a good fight all day. After six and a half hours on the plane and keeping up with Cecile, I figured they could use the recreation.

They took turns getting the best of each other. But just before crying time set in, I pulled one off the other and said, "You both sleep on top. There's enough room."

"Why do you get a bed all to yourself?" Vonetta cried. "You're not that big that you need a bed all to yourself."

I was big enough to give up a full view of the world on the 727 and big enough to outsmart my sisters at every turn.

"You can come down here with me," I said, scooting over so I wasn't claiming the whole bed. "I don't care."

"I'm staying on top," Vonetta said.

"Me too."

We looked around in silence at the walls, the dresser. The goosenecked floor lamp with its half-moon glass bowl. It certainly wasn't much.

Vonetta wanted to say something. She had that look.

"Spit it out, Vonetta," I said.

"Yeah, spit it," Fern said.

Vonetta cut her eyes toward Fern. To me, she said, "Delphine. What we got to do with Mexico?"

That one had also thrown me when Cecile said it: *Should have gone to Mexico to get rid of you when I had the chance.* I didn't rightfully know what that meant, but I was all my sisters had, so I said, "That's where women go who don't want their babies."

"But why Mexico?"

"And not Queens?" Fern asked.

"Because Queens is too close," I said as if I knew. Then I added, showing all of my age and wisdom, "They buy babies down in Mexico for rich people."

They both said, "Oh."

I didn't want to say Big Ma was right. Cecile was no kind of mother. Cecile didn't want us. Cecile was crazy. I didn't have to.

Mean Lady Ming

We stood as one, looking up at her. Me in the front, Vonetta and Fern at my sides. She was tall and broad shouldered, where Pa was just tall. As hungry as I was, all I could think was that they made you dance with a boy in the sixth grade. That I would never look right dancing with a boy, and for that I had Cecile to thank.

I spoke first: "We're hungry."

As usual, my sisters' voices followed on top of mine.

Vonetta: "What's for supper?"

Then Fern: "Hungry. Hungry." She rubbed her belly.

We made a picture. Us looking up at her and her looking down at us. In the animal kingdom the mother bird brings back all she's gathered for the day and drops it into the open mouths of each bird squawking to be fed. Cecile looked at us like it didn't occur to her that we would be hungry and she'd have to do what mothers do: feed their young. I'm no Big Ma in the kitchen, but I would have opened a can of beans and fried up some franks. I can bake a chicken and boil potatoes. I would have never let my long-gone daughters travel nearly three thousand miles without turning on the stove.

She said, "What you want from me?"

"Supper," I answered. "It's past eight o'clock. We haven't had real food since breakfast."

"With Big Ma."

"And Papa."

I kept going. "That was"—I glanced at my wrist—"nine hours and twelve minutes ago."

Vonetta next: "Airline food don't count."

Fern last: "Surely don't."

She was still looking down at us as if we'd thrown a monkey wrench into her quiet Tuesday evening. Then she spoke. "Where's the money your father gave you?"

I crossed my arms. There was no way she was getting our money. "That money's for Disneyland," I told her.

"To go on all the rides."

"And meet Tinker Bell."

This was the first time we heard Cecile laugh, and she laughed like the crazy mother she was turning out to be. "Is Tinker Bell going to feed you?" She was still laughing.

31

We didn't think she was funny. We said nothing rather than talk back and get slapped.

"Look," she said, "if you want to eat, hand over the money."

I stared her down—something I'd never try with Big Ma. Cecile didn't seem to care. She said, "Fine. I got plenty of air sandwiches here. Go on back to the room, open your mouths, and catch one."

The staredown ended right there. I unlaced my right tennis shoe, wriggled my foot out, and removed the mound of tens and twenties Pa had given me. Cecile didn't care that the money had been baking under my foot since we'd left Brooklyn. She took the money, unfolded and counted the bills, then stuffed them in her pants pocket, except for a ten-dollar bill, which she held out to me.

"Go 'round the corner to Ming's. Order a large shrimp lo mein . . ."—she counted our heads as if she didn't know how many of us she'd had—"four egg rolls, and a big bottle of Pepsi."

Vonetta and Fern squealed for the shrimp and Pepsi, forgetting that this was wrong. Our mother should have cooked real food for us—at the very least baked a chicken. Made franks and beans.

"Fruit punch," I said. "Big Ma don't allow us to have strong drinks."

Cecile let out a single whoop of a laugh. Vonetta and

Fern were too excited about having takeout to see that our mother was crazy.

I said, "We have to call Pa. Let him know we arrived."

They chimed in.

"Safe and sound."

"On the ground."

Cecile said, "Phone's next to Ming's."

"You mean you don't have a phone?" Vonetta asked.

Cecile said, "I don't have no one to call, and I don't want no one calling me."

Whether Cecile had a phone was not my main worry. "We have to go out after eight to call Pa and get the food? Aren't you coming with us?"

"Ming's is a couple blocks down Magnolia, around the corner." She pointed the direction. "Phone booth's right there."

When we were barely out the door, she added, "And tell Ming to give you four plates, four forks, four napkins, and four paper cups. No sense dirtying dishes. And you're not coming inside my kitchen!"

We all looked at one another and thought the same thing: crazy.

I led the way in the direction Cecile pointed. Down the walk, past the slumping palm tree, and made a right turn. Vonetta and Fern as usual nipped the heels of my tennis shoes.

It wasn't dark at all, but it wasn't high daylight, either. Kids of all ages still ran around playing in yards and riding bikes on the street. I bet kids ran around and played out here all year long and not only in the summer. We usually went to the summer camp at the Y or drove down to Alabama in Papa's Wildcat.

We came upon some kids playing freeze tag. They jumped from lively wiggle worms to frozen statues just as we neared their yard. We felt the smirks of the gaping statues on us. Vonetta smiled, welcoming their interest in us. She was scouting out new friends to be with for the next twenty-eight days. I let her lag a step or two behind to wink and smile at them. You can't stop Vonetta from chasing after friends.

I kept walking, Fern sticking close to me. Vonetta skipped until she caught up.

One thing was for sure. These blocks might have been long like the blocks on Herkimer Street, but we were far from Brooklyn. I didn't know where any of these streets led, but I walked down Magnolia like I knew where I was going.

I couldn't help but notice that not one yard had a palm tree. Not one. Or stucco. Not one house was painted that crazy green color. I was thinking this when behind us crept a rumbling against concrete, like a barrel rolling, the rolling broken by the cracks in the sidewalk. I turned.

A voice yelled, *"Gangway!"*

We tried to jump aside, but the three of us jumping all together only got us so far.

A boy on top of a wooden board—this flying T with tricycle wheels in the back—rumbled by and managed to clip me good.

"*Hey!* Watch out!" I called after him, shaking my fist.

He only stopped at the corner to pick up his flying T, carry it across the street, and lay it back down on the sidewalk. "Sorry!" he yelled without turning around. Then he gave it a running push and jumped on it, eventually lying stomach down, his arms outstretched as he held on to both ends of the T.

"What was that?" Vonetta asked.

"Some stupid boy," I said. "Come on, y'all."

I had to pull Vonetta's chin away from the direction of the boy on the flying T. She kept looking even after he was long gone.

Ming's was where Cecile said it was. Around the corner and a couple blocks down. There was a big sign, MING'S, and underneath it, red neon characters that looked like fighting men waving swords. The telephone booth was also where Cecile said it would be, right next to Ming's. I planned on calling Pa before getting the food, but the booth was already occupied by a light-skinned guy with a big, floppy Afro. He was turned sideways, but I could see his profile, his beakish nose. The way he pushed his head this way and that, suspiciously, while he talked.

We stood with our arms folded, waiting for him to finish. He looked like a fugitive from justice. I could spot one when I saw one. I love a good crime story, especially *The F.B.I.* Crime shows come on late, and I sneak to catch whatever Big Ma falls asleep watching. That's how this guy looked. Like he was calling his ma to see if the coast was clear to come home without the mob or the coppers on his tail.

He saw us standing with our arms folded and turned his back to us. I got it. He had a lot of dimes and planned to use each one.

We went inside Ming's. We were barely in the restaurant, which wasn't a restaurant, just a counter with a kitchen on the far side and two small tables with benches on our side. The Chinese lady behind the counter said, "No free egg rolls. No more free egg rolls." She waved her hands like "Shoo, stray cat."

I didn't know how to answer. I didn't ask for any free egg rolls. But we were the only ones inside Ming's, and she was staring straight at me.

Vonetta said, "We don't want free egg rolls."

Fern piped in, "We want shrimp lo mein and Pepsi."

Vonetta said, "And four plates, four forks, four napkins, and four cups."

Fern: "And four egg rolls."

Vonetta: "All for money. Not for free."

Finally I said, "It's takeout. To go."

I uncurled the ten-dollar bill to show her. Usually I am Johnny-on-the-spot, speaking up for my sisters and me. But this time I went blank for no reason I could think of. It was nice to have Vonetta and Fern jump right in.

The lady shouted in Chinese to the back of the kitchen. She sounded even meaner than when she'd said "No free egg rolls." I decided that just like Cecile was crazy, the Chinese lady was mean. Mean Lady Ming.

She nodded to us and said, "Okay. Sit."

We sat down and waited. Mean Lady Ming kept talking. "Everybody poor. Everybody hungry. I give free egg roll. Feel sorry. Then everyone come for free egg roll."

She muttered on like Cecile did and looked mean and tired like Big Ma looks on washboard days.

While I was sitting with my sisters, I made up my mind about Oakland. There was nothing and no one in all of Oakland to like. I would get on a plane and fly back to New York if Big Ma showed up wanting her grandbabies. I wouldn't even tell Cecile "Thanks for the visit."

Collect Call

Mean Lady Ming laid a dollar bill and a few coins on the counter. She handed me the brown paper bag with the food, gave Vonetta the bottle of Pepsi and a small bottle of fruit punch, then gave Fern a paper bag with the plates, cups, forks, and napkins. I scooped up all of the change. There were at least two dimes in coins, which was enough to call home to Brooklyn collect.

When we went outside, the beakish guy with the floppy Afro was gone. We all squeezed into the phone booth with our bags from Ming's.

I hooked my finger inside the hole for zero on the phone and dialed. The operator came on and I spoke up.

"Operator, I want to make a collect call to Louis Gaither."

Papa's proper name felt strange coming from my mouth. I said it again clearer although the operator didn't ask me to. Instead, she asked for my name and I gave it to her. "Delphine."

There's nothing mumbly about the way I talk. I don't swallow my letters or run them together. The operator still asked, "Can I have that again?" as if she didn't get it the first time. I broke it into syllables. "Del-FEEN."

She told me to stay on the line. While she was ringing Pa, I realized my Timex was still on Brooklyn time and that it was after eleven o'clock. Pa rose in the dark for work and was asleep by nine. I started to wind the stem when the operator came back. "Go ahead, Miss."

"Hello? Hello?" Big Ma sounded far away, but we heard her and were glad to have reached home.

Already Vonetta and Fern began puppy yelping in the background and grabbing at the phone. I gave them a stern look to make them quit it. Before I could say "We're here in Oakland with Cecile," Big Ma said, "Delphine! Do you know how much this phone call is costing your father?"

There was no time to be tongue-tied. I spoke up. "But Papa said call."

"Not collect, Delphine. Where'd you get a thought like that? I knew you girls should have never left Brooklyn. You fly out to Oakland and lose your last ounce of common sense. Let me speak to your mother."

"She's not here," I said. "She's in her house."

Vonetta and Fern were still shouting to Big Ma and Papa, who had to be asleep.

"And why are you out in the street in the middle of the night? I'm going to tell your pa about this." Big Ma scolded and fussed, running up the phone bill even higher. When she was done telling me about myself and about that "no kind of mother, Cecile," I told her we were safe and said good night, and Vonetta and Fern hollered out, "Good night, Big Ma! And Pa!" Then I hung up the phone.

At least I had done what Pa had told me to do. I called.

Cecile guarded the kitchen's swinging door and pointed us to the living room, where she had laid out a waxy tablecloth on the floor. We spread out around the cloth. Cecile took over everything, dumping shrimp lo mein and an egg roll on each plate, tossing everyone a fork and a napkin.

To me she said, "Pour the drinks," which I did. This was the most mothering we got, if you don't count her coming to claim us. Not that I wanted or needed any mothering. I was just thinking about Vonetta and Fern. They were expecting a mother. At least a hug. A "Look at how y'all have grown." A look of sorrow and a plea for forgiveness. I knew better.

At least that was one thing Cecile and Big Ma had in common. Big Ma had no forgiveness for Cecile, and Cecile had no need for it.

Mean Lady Ming had thrown in a pair of chopsticks. Vonetta and Fern eyed the wooden sticks and formulated ideas about turning them into hairpins, play-fight swords, and pickup sticks. Cecile ended all of that when she broke the sticks joined at the top, rubbed them against each other like she was kindling twigs for a campfire, then wrapped noodles around them and shoved the noodles, shrimp, and sticks into her mouth.

We were all staring. We'd never seen anyone eating with chopsticks other than on TV. We'd never seen colored people eating with them, and here was our mother eating with chopsticks like the Chinese men that I had read about who worked on the railroads. She ate hungrily, setting no type of table-manner examples for us, her daughters.

Cecile knew our eyes were on her. With a mouthful of food she said, "Thought y'all were hungry."

We picked up our forks and ate.

When we were done, Cecile grabbed everything that hadn't been used—soy sauce, spicy mustard, her fork, an extra cup that Mean Lady Ming had thrown in. She told us to stay right there while she brought everything into the kitchen. So we stayed put.

I thought she might want to talk to us. Find out how

we were doing in school. What we liked and didn't like. If we ever had chicken pox or our tonsils taken out. While I thought about what I'd tell her, we heard a knock on the door. Then another loud knock. We jumped up to look through the curtains, but Cecile came out of the kitchen.

"Get back in the room. Get."

And we did. But I had caught a glimpse through the curtain. I had already seen three people in dark clothes with Afros.

FOR the People

We were trained spies back in Brooklyn. Scrunched together, pressing our ears to the door, wall, or air, we used hand signals and mouthed words instead of whispered. If necessary I could shush my sisters with a glare to bottle up their loose giggling. You can't giggle and be a spy.

It was by pressing our ears to the air that we had heard Pa say, "No, Ma. They need to know her, and she needs to know them. They're flying to Oakland. That's final." It had been all we could do not to let on when Pa sat us down the next morning.

The knock on the door, Cecile ordering us to hide in our room, and her clearing away all evidence of us were not actions of a mother. These were actions of a secret

43

agent. Or a fugitive from justice. Someone who doesn't open her door wide and welcoming like Big Ma does when the doorbell rings. Hers were the actions of someone who wears hats, scarves, and shades to keep from being recognized. Kind of like the guy in the phone booth. Someone obviously hiding out.

Once again, we fell into our spying positions, angling ourselves at the cracked door to see, while pressing our ears against the air. From there we could see pieces of the three figures who entered Cecile's house. All wore dark colors. One had on a black jacket and a black beret. The other two, black T-shirts and black berets over Afros. We steadied our heavy, excited breathing to hear what we could.

It wasn't long after greeting one another that their talking turned to arguing. It was their voices, all three of them against hers. It sounded like:

"Seize the time."

"For the people."

"The time is now."

Versus her:

"Me . . ."

"My . . ."

"No . . ."

"No . . ."

Then each one of them firing off:

"The people . . ."

44

"The people . . ."

"The people . . ."

Against her:

"My art."

"My work."

"My time. My materials. My printing press."

"Me. My. No. No."

I was sure they were Black Panthers. They were on the news a lot lately. The Panthers on TV said they were in communities to protect poor black people from the powerful; to provide things like food, clothing, and medical help; and to fight racism. Even so, most people were afraid of Black Panthers because they carried rifles and shouted "Black Power." From what I could see, these three didn't have rifles, and Cecile didn't seem afraid. Just annoyed because they wanted her things but she didn't want to give them. Big Ma said God could not have made a being more selfish than Cecile. At least she was like that with everyone, not just us.

Cecile said, "Paper isn't free. Ink isn't free. My printing press isn't free. I'm not free."

One of them answered, "None of us is free, Sister Inzilla. Eldridge Cleaver isn't free. Huey Newton isn't free. H. Rap Brown isn't free. Muhammad Ali isn't free."

I knew he meant her, Cecile, when he said Inzilla. I didn't know some of those other names. Only Huey Newton, the Black Panther leader, and Muhammad Ali, who used to be Cassius Clay. I guessed the others were Black Panthers or black people who were in prison. I knew Ali had refused to go to Vietnam and fight like Uncle Darnell was doing. I still didn't get what any of that had to do with Cecile.

Another one said, "That's why everyone must contribute to the cause."

The third voice added, "Like Huey said, 'We should all carry the weight, and those who have extreme abilities will have to carry extremely heavy loads.'"

There were words thrown back and forth. Long, unfamiliar words ending in *tion*, *ism*, and *actic*, with more talk about "the people" thrown in for good measure, like Big Ma throwing a pinch of salt into the cake batter.

They weren't just talking. The three Black Panthers were rapping. Laying it down. Telling it like it is, like talking was their weapon. Their words versus her words. Hers falling, theirs rising. When her voice fell as low as she would allow it, she stamped her foot and said, "All right. All right. But you gotta take my kids." And shortly after, they were gone.

We retreated from the door and jumped on the top daybed. This was the next part after the spy missions. Pooling together what we'd learned.

Vonetta asked, "Is she giving us away?"

Then Fern: "To those people?"

I shook my head no. "She couldn't explain that to Papa."

"Or to Big Ma," Fern said.

"Then who were those people?" Vonetta asked.

"In the black clothes."

"Telling her to carry the weight."

"Talk, talk, talking, on and on and on," Fern said.

"They're Black Panthers. They're probably who she's running from."

Vonetta asked, "Who are the Black Panthers?"

"You know. Like Frieda's brother." I made the Black Power sign with my fist. Only Big Ma and I watch the news. Big Ma enjoys hearing about all the trouble going on in the world. It isn't that she actually likes it. She just needs to hear about everything and talk about it. Since Pa works all day and is tired at night, Big Ma gives me her opinions while I wash dishes. You name it. President LBJ. Ho Chi Minh in North Vietnam. Martin Luther King's funeral. Bobby Kennedy's funeral. The race riots. The sit-ins. Elizabeth Taylor's next husband. The Black Panthers. Each holds Big Ma's interest.

"It has something to do with Cecile's paper," I said.

"And her ink," Vonetta said.

"And the people," Fern said.

We couldn't imagine what tied all three things together. Then Vonetta suggested, "Maybe they want her to write a poem."

"About the people," Fern said.

"Using her special inks and papers," Vonetta said.

Pa had told us Cecile wrote poems, but I'd already known that. Flashes of Cecile chanting words, tapping a rhythm with her pencil, then writing. And Uncle Darnell had said I was always there, quiet, in the kitchen while she chanted, tapped, and wrote. I'd get those flashing pictures. But in pieces.

Vonetta asked, "Can they make you write poems?" Then Vonetta fixed her voice deep like a man's. "You better write a poem about the people, or else."

Fern and I laughed at her. She loved entertaining us.

"They don't send the Black Panthers to your house to make you write a poem," I said.

Vonetta's eyes lit up fox bright. She had an idea.

"Cecile prints up her own money. How else do you think she got this house? Cecile is printing her own money in the kitchen. That's why we can't go in there and that's why she didn't cook fried chicken."

"Or 'nana pudding."

I shook my head. "With all the money she'd have to print up to buy this house, the FBI would have tracked her down and thrown her in the pokey."

"The pokey!" That made Fern laugh. Then Vonetta and Fern started dancing and singing: "You do the hokey pokey and you turn yourself around. That's what it's all about."

Glass of Water

If we were at home with Pa and Big Ma, we would have been bathed and in bed an hour and five minutes ago. But we weren't in Brooklyn. We were in Oakland with Cecile.

I glanced at my trusty Timex. I wasn't mad that Vonetta had gotten the Timex with the pink wristband and couldn't hold on to it, while mine is plain brown and still on my arm. My brown leather wristband is just fine. It's the clock part that matters anyway. I can count on it to keep things running on schedule.

Its waterproof face told me what I needed to know at nine thirty-five in the evening. That it took three minutes for warm water and a handful of Tide soap powder to make the right amount of suds. Fifteen minutes was enough time for the day's dirt to fall to the bottom of the tub, while Vonetta and Fern styled bubble beehive hairdos on their heads and beards on each other. But give them one minute longer and I'd end up pulling Fern off of Vonetta and mopping up sops of water splashed onto the bathroom tiles.

After I got my sisters in, out, dried, and lotioned, I took my bath, setting my watch on the porcelain edge to keep an eye on my own twelve minutes in the tub. The watch part might have been waterproof, but the plain brown leather band didn't care for soap and hot water. Bathwater made the leather hard and clammy against my skin. I always took it off.

Only when I sat in the tub did I wish my Timex wasn't so reliable or the ticking so steady. Oh, how I wished the minute hand would slow down and give me time for a nice, long soak. Wish all I wanted, I couldn't leave Vonetta and Fern alone to sort out who'd sleep at what end of the daybed. Three extra minutes in the tub and I'd be sorry. I stuck to the schedule.

We were in our summer nighties. Vonetta and Fern lay side by side, their elbows propped up on the higher bed, while I sat on the lower bed. Fern's eyelids grew droopy. Still, she yawned and demanded story time.

I opened *Peter Pan*, one of the books I'd checked out for a two-week loan before we'd left Brooklyn. I had it all worked out and counted the pages I'd read each night, dividing that by twenty-eight days. I had two dollars and eighty cents in my drawer at home to pay for the late fees for the remaining two weeks when we returned to Brooklyn.

This *Peter Pan* was better than the *Peter Pan* coloring books at home. It was a real book, thick with more than one hundred pages of adventure. Vonetta and Fern were soon under the spell of Peter and Wendy flying like fairies. Both Vonetta and Fern gave out three pages sooner than I had planned. I put my bookmark—a coaster from the airplane—in the right spot and pulled the blanket over my sisters.

As quiet as a spy, I unbuckled my suitcase and took out my borrowed copy of *Island of the Blue Dolphins.* I turned off the goosenecked floor lamp and sat in the hallway, where light beamed from the living room. Cecile was in her kitchen doing whatever she did in there.

I fell asleep with my book in my lap. What woke me was a thump. Through clouded, sleepy eyes, I made out the back of Fern's ruffled nightie. Her little heels were headed to Cecile's kitchen. I shook myself awake and jumped to my feet. As sure as I knew Cecile was crazy and unmotherly, I knew I must stop Fern.

It was too late. I wasn't fast enough to catch hold of Fern's nightie. Cecile was right there, guarding whatever she was hiding in her kitchen.

Sleepy and sweet voiced, Fern asked, "Can I have a glass of water?"

Papa could never bring himself to say no to Fern. He left that to Big Ma, Vonetta, and me. But Cecile said, "Drank the water in the bathroom."

"It's nasty," Fern said.

"Then you ain't thirsty, little girl."

"I'm not Little Girl. I'm Fern."

"She didn't mean . . ." My mouth sped to Fern's rescue, but Cecile's raised hand stopped me. I got the message, and she lowered her stop sign.

"Let's get one thing straight, Little Girl. No one's going in my kitchen."

It's hard to believe the last time they'd seen each other, Fern had been a loaf of bread in Cecile's arms. That was how Uncle Darnell told it to me. Some pieces of it I even remember. How Cecile had nursed Fern, burped her, and placed her in her crib before leaving us. It's funny that Cecile had at least thought to give Fern a last drink, but all the same left Fern wanting her milk. Now they stood across from each other: Cecile towering over Fern with her arms crossed, and Fern looking up at Cecile. Fern balled both fists, banging them against her sides like she usually did before she jumped on Vonetta.

I took one of Fern's fists in my hand and eased it flat. Then I put on my "talking to white folks" voice and said,

"Can you get her a glass of cold water?"

I'm used to doing what's hard. Like three days' worth of homework in one night to catch up from being out of school sick. Like forty-six push-ups in sixty seconds to win a bet with a boy. Like standing mean mouthed over Vonetta and Fern until they swallow a tablespoon each of hard pine cough syrup. But saying "please" without actually saying it to someone you don't want to say "please" to in the first place tops the list of hard.

When Cecile raised her hand, I pushed Fern back, not knowing if she raised her hand only to point down at Fern. I didn't know Cecile yet. I didn't know how mean or crazy she was.

She said, "Stay out there." Then she backed into the kitchen muttering, "Didn't ask no one to send you here, no way."

When the door had swung, I heard a rustle between the flash of opening and closing. Like fall leaves rustling. I looked up in time to see white wings hanging from above in the quick flash of the opened door.

To the normal kids in my classroom, that would have looked crazy. White wings hanging in the kitchen. But I remembered strange things that got me laughed at in school. Things about Cecile. I'd been dumb enough to volunteer facts about my mother for show-and-tell. "My mother writes on cereal boxes and on the wall," I'd said proudly in the second grade. And this, the white wings

53

hanging in her house, wasn't strange at all. It was halfway what I'd expected. I would hate to think she had left us to lead a normal, cookie-baking, pork chop–frying life.

The sink ran full force. I heard opening and slamming. Metal banging against the countertop maybe. Cracking and shaking. The rock crackling of ice in a metal tray. More opening and slamming again. Fern clung to my side and then inched behind me.

Cecile came out holding the extra paper cup from Mean Lady Ming's. Seeing Fern hiding behind me, she said, "It's too late for all of that. Here. Take it."

Fern stayed put, so I went to take the cup. Cecile pulled back, spilling a few drops at her feet.

"Little Girl, you better take this if you want it."

Fern's fists balled from behind her nightie and again I reached out, but Cecile glared, like, *Girl, I will knock you down.*

Fern stepped from behind me and took the cup from Cecile's hand. "I'm not Little Girl. I'm Fern."

"Well, you better drink this cup of ice water, Little Girl. Every last drop."

Fern drank it all down without stopping. Probably to prove she could. Probably to not stand near Cecile any longer than she had to. Then she handed me the cup with ice, and I returned it to Cecile.

As many times as Big Ma said it, I never fully believed it. That no one, not even Cecile, needed to have their way so badly or was so selfish. That she could leave Pa, Vonetta, Fern, and me over something as small and silly as a name. That Cecile left because Pa wouldn't let her pick out Fern's name. But I saw and heard it with my own ears and eyes. She refused to call Fern by her name, and that made Big Ma right about Cecile.

INSEPARABLE

"If you girls want breakfast, go'n down to the People's Center."

We said all together, "The People's Center?"

Without skipping a beat Cecile said, "Next to the library on Adeline. Just keep walking till you see kids and old people lined up."

"You're not going to take us?" I didn't mean it to worm out as a question and was mad at myself for asking instead of stating.

"You don't need me to walk down the street. The park is on the other side. Y'all can run around after breakfast or stay for the program at the Center. It don't make me no difference."

Cecile pointed a fountain pen at me. Two more pens were stuck in her hair. "You the oldest. You can read street signs."

Vonetta, indignant, said, "I can read street signs too."

"Me too."

Instead of saying "I didn't ask for all of that" like I expected, Cecile smacked her palm against her thigh and said, "Then that settles it. Step out this door, cross the street, keep going a block till you get to Adeline. If you can read, you can't miss the *A* in 'Adeline.' Turn left. Keep walking till you see the library. Center's on the same block. Can't miss it. Nothing but black folks in black clothes rapping revolution and a line of hungry black kids."

Then she cut herself off from us, tapped her fountain pen, and repeated, "Black folks, in black clothes, rapping revolution."

We had Black Panthers in Brooklyn. Black Panther posters with SEIZE THE TIME stapled onto telephone poles. We just never had any Black Panthers marching down Herkimer Street, knocking on our door demanding that we give to the cause or calling us some kind of Sister name we had never heard of.

My sisters and I didn't make a move toward the door. We couldn't believe our ears. Our crazy mother was sending us outside to find militant strangers if we wanted to eat.

She said, "Wait." I hoped she had changed her mind

about us going to the Center. She went into the kitchen and came out with a cardboard box, a little smaller than the shoe box for Papa's work boots. "Here," she said. "Take this to the Center. Give it to the Panthers. Tell them it's from Inzilla." That's what I thought she said. Inzilla.

She put the box in my hands.

"Who do I—"

"Just find a black beret. Any black beret will do. Make sure you tell them I gave to the cause. You tell them, 'Don't come knocking on my door asking for my materials.'"

I knew I wouldn't be telling no Black Panthers what Cecile said. That she gave to the cause and not to come knocking on her door for her stuff. I just took the box and nodded, because that's how you treat crazy people. You nod and count down twenty-seven days for crazy to come to an end.

Vonetta and Fern looked to me for what to do next, and Cecile noticed this. There was no lip smile from Cecile, but her eyes found it funny that they always looked to me first.

"Come on," I said. "Let's go get breakfast."

We were about to leave, but Fern stopped cold. Her eyes bugged out and she balled her fists. "Wait! Wait!"

Vonetta and I waited while she ran into the back room, her steps all buffalo stomps. I didn't mind Fern's stomping because it annoyed Cecile that her house had been invaded by our mouths, wants, and feet. It served her right.

Both Vonetta and I knew why Fern ran back to the room. We'd been seeing this go on for years. Fern returned with Miss Patty Cake in tow. From her look of disgust, I believed Cecile would have spat on her own floor if she wouldn't have had to clean it up.

"Aren't you too big to be dragging that thing with you?"

As far as I was concerned, Cecile had nothing to say about Fern and Miss Patty Cake. Miss Patty Cake was there when Cecile wasn't.

Now I smiled. I'd understood that Fern and Miss Patty Cake were like that Nat King Cole song "Unforgettable." When I'd first heard his satiny smooth voice sing "Like a song of love that clings to me," I knew Miss Patty Cake was like that song of love to Fern.

Cecile thought Fern would buckle under a seven-year-old's shame. When Fern didn't answer, she asked again, "Aren't you too big for alla that?"

Fern shook four braids and barrettes and said, "No," taking delight in answering no for no's sake. No, because Cecile didn't have a hug and a kiss that Fern expected. No, because Cecile didn't leap up and get that cold glass of water. No, because Cecile had yet to call Fern, Fern.

Vonetta groaned. She had fought enough name-callers on behalf of Miss Patty Cake. I had fought my share too, but so what. It was for Fern and her doll. Except for going to school and church, Fern and Miss Patty Cake had been inseparable for as long as Fern or anyone else could remember.

Cecile shook like we had given her the willies. She probably asked herself, *Who are these kids?*

There was no use in standing around for a long farewell and a list of dos and don'ts. We weren't leaving Big Ma. We were leaving Cecile with her kitchen and her palm tree. And just as I felt we had gotten the last lick by turning and going, Cecile said, "Don't kill yourself to get back here. Stay out till sundown."

We walked along the street, a moving triangle. Me in the front. Vonetta and Fern with Miss Patty Cake behind me at both sides.

"I wanna go home."

"Me too."

I knew which home they meant. I said, "We're going back home in twenty-seven days."

"Let's call Papa," Vonetta said.

"And Big Ma."

I said, "Not yet. Big Ma hasn't gotten over the collect call from yesterday. We gotta get up enough dimes to make a real call across the country."

Vonetta said, "We should call Papa. Tell him she's mean."

"And she don't want us."

"And she won't cook or let us in the kitchen."

"To get a cold glass of water."

"In her kitchen."

"In her house."

I said, "We will. Just not yet."

Vonetta said, "If Big Ma knew . . ."

"And Papa."

"They'd be here lightning quick to get us."

"Yeah. Quick like lightning."

I said, "We'll need a lot of dimes."

Breakfast Program

We found the Center like Cecile said we would. A line of hungry kids waited for breakfast, except they weren't all black. There were older teens in mostly black clothes and Afros posted like soldiers guarding the outside. That hardly seemed necessary when a white-and-black police car circled around the block.

Vonetta was already smiling and showing anyone who'd look her way that she was worth a smile back. She had picked out three girls who looked alike enough to be sisters, each one as thick as my sisters and I were lanky. They wore white boots and daisy dresses with flared sleeves. They might as well have been going to a go-go, not to a free breakfast.

I kept Fern near, my arms crossed before me. I was here to make sure my sisters and I ate breakfast, and to stay out of Cecile's hair. If Vonetta wanted to get her feelings hurt chasing after smiles and go-go boots, that was on her.

The Panthers opened the doors and we trailed inside, the three of us sticking close together. As we entered, I did what Cecile said. I handed the box to the first Black Panther I saw and said, "This is from Cecile." I wasn't about to call her some name I didn't know or tell them she said to leave her alone. The Black Panther guy opened the box. He took out a sheet from a stack of paper—a flyer with a crouching black panther and some writing on it—and held it up to examine it. He nodded, said, "Thank you, Sister," and took the box with him.

The three girls in the flower dresses were standing on line looking at us. Vonetta tried to steer me over to them, but I didn't want to go chasing after them. Their dresses looked so nice and new. We wore shorts and sun tops, although Oakland wasn't as sunny as we'd imagined California would be. I found us a place on line behind Puerto Ricans who didn't look Puerto Rican but who spoke Spanish. Then I remembered our study of the fifty states. They were probably Mexicans.

I thought Black Panthers would only look out for black people, but there were the two Mexicans, a little white boy, and a boy who looked both black and Chinese. Everyone else was black. I'd never seen the Black Panthers making breakfast on the news. But then, beating eggs never makes the evening news.

As we stood on line, a guy who should have kept walking stopped right in front of us. He crossed his arms and looked down at Fern.

I recognized the beakish nose on that narrow face. He was the one in the telephone booth who had turned his back to us, like he didn't want to be seen. For all I knew, he was one of those in the black berets and Afros who'd come knocking on Cecile's door last night. Now he stood across from Fern, his legs apart and his arms folded.

"What is wrong with this picture," he stated instead of asked. He knew the answer, all right. I was pretty good at reading faces.

He didn't have a leather jacket, but he was one of them. On his black T-shirt was a dead white pig with flies buzzing around it and the words OFF THE PIG in white letters. His hair was a big loose Afro because it was a little stringy. Stringy like Lucy Raleigh's, who bragged about being part Chickasaw in the fourth grade but by fifth grade was singing "I'm Black and I'm Proud" louder than loud because James Brown's song had made it the thing to do.

The stringy-Afro-wearing beak man wasn't Papa-grown or Cecile-grown. Probably all of nineteen or twenty, but he thought he was something. He was putting on a show for all the other black beret wearers.

When none of us spoke, he pointed and asked again the

question whose answer he already knew. "What is wrong with this picture?"

Fern pointed back at him and said, "I don't know. What's wrong with this picture?"

The other Black Panthers laughed and told Fern, "That's right, Li'l Sis. Don't take nothing from no one." And they slapped palms and said stuff like "These are Sister Inzilla's, all right. Look at them."

Beak Man tried to stand up to his humiliation. Shake it off.

"Li'l Sis, are you a white girl or a black girl?"

Fern said, "I'm a colored girl."

He didn't like the sound of "colored girl." He said, "Black girl."

Fern said, "Colored."

"Black girl."

Vonetta and I threw our "colored" on top of Fern's like we were ringtossing at Coney Island. This was bigger than *Say it loud, I'm Black and I'm proud.* If one of us said "colored," we all said "colored." Unless we were fighting among ourselves.

"All right, then. 'Cullid' girls," Big Beak said, "why are you carrying that self-hatred around in your arms?"

An older teenage girl in a Cal State T-shirt said, "Kelvin, you're crazy. Leave those colored girls alone."

Big-beaked, stringy-haired Kelvin looked pleased with himself.

I said, "That's not self-hatred. That's her doll."

"Yeah. A doll baby."

"Miss Patty Cake."

In spite of the Cal State girl and the other Black Panthers saying leave those girls alone, he went on.

"Are your eyes blue like hers? Is your hair blond like hers? Is your skin white like hers?"

The girl said again, "Crazy Kelvin, stop it. Just stop it."

Crazy Kelvin turned to a lady who wore an African-print dress and a matching cloth wrapped around her head. "Sister Mukumbu. Our 'colored' girls here need some reeducation." And he walked away, one of those pimp walks, like *How you like me now*?

Sister Mukumbu just smiled at him like she didn't take Crazy Kelvin seriously. She and the Cal State girl exchanged a look.

The Cal State girl turned toward me and said, "Don't mind Crazy Kelvin. That's what we call him. He's a little wild."

For all of that, the eggs were cold, but we ate them, along with the buttered toast and orange slices. It was better than eating air sandwiches at Cecile's.

Fern hugged Miss Patty Cake but refrained from putting a piece of toast to her doll's lips like she would have done at home. Still, the other kids laughed at her and called her White Baby Lover and Big Baby, except for the boy who looked both colored and Chinese. I told them to shut up. And that went for the three sisters in flower dresses. Even the tallest sister. No one could call Fern White Baby Lover even though Miss Patty Cake was a white baby and Fern loved her. No one could call Fern a Big Baby but Vonetta and me. Vonetta ate her toast silently. We had cost Vonetta her summer friends with the white go-go boots and happening dresses. But I didn't care. Fern could love Miss Patty Cake all she wanted. We could call ourselves Vanilla Wafers, Chocolate Chips, or Oreo Cookies for all I cared about black girls and colored girls.

And even though Cecile didn't bother to bring us here or stick up for Fern, the Black Panthers had slapped palms and said, "Those are Sister Inzilla's, all right."

Even the Earth Is a Revolutionary

Once breakfast was over, most of the kids left, except for a dozen who stayed behind, including us. I told my sisters we might as well stick around for the summer camp program. Cecile had made it clear she didn't want to see us anytime soon, so we told Sister Mukumbu our names and followed her and Sister Pat, the young woman in the Cal State T-shirt, into a classroom.

I felt silly and wrong calling a grown person Brother So-and-So or Sister Such-and-Such, but thanks to Cecile, we now had brothers and sisters we had never before laid eyes on. Sure, they said "brutha" and "sistah" in Brooklyn, but here it was more of a title and not like you were saying "him" or "her." As far as I could tell, none of the grown people at the Center went by Mr., Mrs., or Miss. If Big Ma could see how quickly our home training had flown out the window, she would have had us on the next Boeing 727 back to New York.

There was something welcoming about Sister Mukumbu, whom I liked right away. If Sister Mukumbu had met us at the airport, we would have felt welcomed as she stepped forward to claim us. She would have wrapped us up in her green, purple, and orange African print dress and begged our forgiveness for having left us.

We sat at one of the two long tables. The classroom was unlike any I had ever been in. Instead of pictures of George Washington, Abraham Lincoln, and President Johnson, there was a picture of Huey Newton sitting in a big wicker chair with a rifle at his side. There were other pictures of mostly black men and a few women hung up around the room. I expected to find Dr. Martin Luther King's photograph hanging on the wall, but I was disappointed. Malcolm X and Muhammad Ali were the only faces I could name. I didn't know any of the women, although one woman looked just like Big Ma. Next to her picture were the words "I'm sick and tired of being sick and tired."

On the walls were big sheets of lined-ruled paper written in teacher's neat handwriting. The first one said "What We Want" in green letters. On the other side of the wall, another said "What We Believe."

Vonetta didn't seem to care that we were in some sort of Black Panther summer camp, learning to become Black Panthers. Her attention was fixed on the three sisters with the flared-sleeve dresses and their round, curly Afros. I knew I would hear all about it later. How it was time for her to have a new hairstyle and that our clothes were baby clothes.

Sister Mukumbu said, "Hirohito Woods."

A boy from the other table with dark spiky hair, brown coppery skin, and slanted eyes groaned. He was probably my age.

Sister Mukumbu smiled in spite of his groaning. She beckoned him to her side, her many bracelets jangling as she waved him forward. "Hirohito will help with my demonstration."

I didn't have to turn to see Vonetta's mile-long pout. It was just like Vonetta to be envious of someone else being in the spotlight. Hirohito didn't seem thrilled. He pushed his chair backward, scraping the floor, and went sullenly up to the front. It was only from the back of his spiky head that I recognized him as the flying T board rider who'd nearly mowed us down yesterday. I had half a mind to sock him good.

Sister Mukumbu said, "I'm going to be the sun, and Hirohito will be the earth." She leaned and whispered something in his ear. He heaved a big sigh, like he didn't want to do whatever it was she told him but would do it anyway. The sighing was for us kids so he didn't come off as some kind of teacher's pet.

Sister Mukumbu nodded and said firmly, "Now, Hirohito."

He heaved another sigh and began to turn around slowly, each time taking a step to travel around Sister Mukumbu, who stood still and smiled. This was better than socking him in the arm. Watching him turn around and around in his black and silver Raiders jersey. He looked down and probably felt silly. All the kids in the program, including my sisters and me, giggled. Sister Mukumbu wasn't bothered by our giggling or by Hirohito's sighing. She said, "The earth turns slowly on its axis, while also spinning around the sun. Day wouldn't change to night if the earth didn't spin on its axis. The seasons wouldn't change if the earth didn't travel around the sun. This means vegetation wouldn't grow, which means poor farmers couldn't harvest, and poor people couldn't eat if the earth didn't spin on its axis and travel around the sun. That one body spinning in motion affects everyone's lives. Does anyone know another word for the earth's constant spinning?"

That was how I knew Sister Mukumbu was a real teacher, aside from her welcoming smile and her blackboard penmanship. She asked a teacher's type of question. The kind that says: Join in.

Thanks to my time spent with Merriam Webster, I had a few words in mind. *Rotating. Orbiting. Turning. Circling.*

I wanted to join in, but I felt silly, being one of the older kids. Not as silly as Hirohito spinning around but too old to wave my hand frantically as all the younger kids around me were doing. The older sister of the three girls also sat on her answer. She probably knew too but left it up to her sisters, who wanted to be called on.

When one of the kids called out "Revolving," Sister Mukumbu clapped her hands. Her bangles jangled. "Yes! All of your words are right, but 'revolving' is right on!" Sister Pat then gave the boy a cookie.

Sister Mukumbu said, "Revolving. Revolution. Revolutionary. Constant turning. Making things change."

Sister Pat said, "Huey Newton is a revolutionary. Huey makes change."

And Sister Mukumbu continued, saying, "Che Guevara was a revolutionary. Che made change."

As they named all of the revolutionaries who made change, Hirohito came to a complete stop. He held out his hands, a dizzy Frankenstein, and staggered to his chair. The boy who won the cookie said, "Nice spinning, Twinkle Toes." Hirohito rested his head on the table and closed his eyes.

I just thought, Serves you right.

Sister Mukumbu announced, "Today we're going to be like the earth, spinning around and affecting many. Today we're going to think about our part in the revolution."

Vonetta's hand shot up. I kicked her under the table,

but she was determined to have everyone look at her, which meant have everyone look at us. I forgot all about Hirohito and was now afraid of what Vonetta would say next; and sure enough, Vonetta said, "We didn't come for the revolution. We came for breakfast." Then Fern added, "And to meet our mother in Oakland."

If Hirohito's spinning made us giggle, Vonetta's declaration made everyone—except my sisters and me, and the still-dizzy Hirohito—full-out laugh. The group of girls whom Vonetta had been winking at were the main cacklers. Even Sister Mukumbu, caught off guard by Vonetta's and Fern's outbursts, allowed herself a chuckle.

I blamed Vonetta and not Fern, since I didn't want the world to learn we didn't rightfully know our mother. Fern wouldn't have uttered a word if Vonetta hadn't raised her hand to speak. Even worse, Vonetta had thrown a king-sized monkey wrench into my plans. I had hoped to ask Sister Mukumbu about the name the Black Panthers called Cecile and why they called her that. I didn't know exactly how I would have asked her, but something made me believe she would know and that she wouldn't make me feel bad for asking. She certainly wouldn't have given me that "Oh, you poor motherless girl" pity look. Or the snooty "Don't you even know your own mother's name?" Sister Mukumbu would have given me the plain, pure, teacherly truth.

Then Vonetta raised her hand and opened her mouth

and had the world looking and laughing at us. Except for the boy who was too dizzy to laugh. I wasn't about to add fuel to the fire by asking questions about things that I should know, like my mother's name.

CRazy MotheR MountaiN

After the program ended for the day, we stayed out as long as we could. By six o'clock we were hungry. Whether she liked it or not, Cecile had to let us inside her green stucco house. When she opened the door, all she said was "Ya back?" Then she spread the tablecloth on the floor and brought out shrimp lo mein and egg rolls from the kitchen. She had probably gone out to Mean Lady Ming's while we were at the Center.

We washed up and sat Indian-style around the food. I said the blessing and then I asked, "Why the Black Panthers call you Inzilla?" No use letting my curiosity go itching. If I had to ask someone, I might as well go straight to the mountain. The crazy mother mountain.

She gave me a blank stare. Like I said something wrong. Then she corrected me.

"Nzila."

In place of shrugs, my sisters and I shot one another glances. That was not a Brooklyn sound. Or an Alabama sound. It was probably not even an honest-to-goodness Oakland sound.

Instead of trying it out I said, "Why they call you that?"

My sisters followed.

"Isn't your name Cecile?"

"Yeah. Cecile."

She said, "My name is Nzila. Nzila is a poet's name. My poems blow the dust off surfaces to make clear and true paths. Nzila."

I gave her a plain stare. Plain and blank. It might as well have been an eye roll. She probably hated my father's plain face on me. That the plain way about him was the plain way about me. I didn't know about blowing dust and clearing paths. I knew about hot-combing thick heads of hair and ironing pleated wool skirts for school.

She said, "It's Yoruba for 'the path.'"

I knew better than to roll my eyes at her "so-called" name and where she said it came from. Instead I asked her where Your Ruba was. She quickly told me it was a people. A nation. In the land of our ancestors.

Vonetta asked, "You mean Prattville, Alabama?"

This time I wouldn't kick Vonetta. Good old Vonetta. Prattville was where Papa and Big Ma were originally from. They weren't from big-city Mobile, Montgomery, or Selma, but from Prattville. And truth be told, my daddy and my grandmama came from a one-cow town rubbing next to Prattville. They just said Prattville because it was more known.

I asked, "So you can change your name any time you want to?"

Vonetta: "To anything you want to?"

Fern: "To anything you can spell?"

Cecile said, "It's my name. My self. I can name my self. And if I'm not the one I was but am now a new self, why would I call my self by an old name?"

Then I said, "If you keep changing your name, how will people know you or your poems?" When my sisters and I speak, one right after the other, it's like a song we sing, a game we play. We never need to pass signals. We just fire off rat-a-tat-tat-tat. Delphine. Vonetta. Fern.

Me: "S'pose you got famous. For writing poems?"

Vonetta: "Then everyone knew your name."

Fern: "And you couldn't hide."

She said, "My poems aren't about that. Fame-seeking poems. They're the people's art," although yesterday she didn't want to have anything to do with "the people."

I said, "What if all the people could recite all of your poems?"

77

Vonetta: "And they said them on the radio."

Fern: "And you became famous."

Me: "You couldn't hide then."

Fern: "Surely couldn't."

She said, "Who you all working for? I think y'all working for the Man undercover. The FBI. The COINTELPRO."

I knew about the FBI from the Sunday night show and from the news, but who were the COINTELPRO? Cecile knew she had us baffled and took control of the talk like she had grabbed both the ball and the jacks.

"Oh, they're slick, all right," she said. "The feds hire midgets to front as kids. They infiltrate families with long-lost cousins who don't look a thing like you, but you take them in because that's how colored folks do; and before you can say "Way down home," your long-lost kin are documenting your every move for their weekly secret meetings with the Man."

"Family don't tell on family," I said.

"Not real family."

"Surely don't."

"That's what you think," Cecile said. She went after Vonetta first because Vonetta was needy in a way that Fern and I weren't. Her eyes stayed wide and fearful. "They get you alone. Alone and scared. They say, 'Vonetta Gaither. Do you love your country? Do you love your father? Your sisters? Your uncle Darnell in Vietnam and Big Ma in Brooklyn?'" At Fern, she aimed, "'Little Girl, do you love your doll baby? Do you love Captain Kangaroo? Your kin-nygarden teacher, graham crackers, and story time? Well, if you want to keep all that safe, tell us all you know about the person named Cecile Johnson, also known as your mother.'"

Fern said her name was not Little Girl. That she was going into the second grade and that she watched *Mighty Mouse* and not *Captain Kangaroo*.

Before Cecile got to me I said, "They don't ask kids nothing. No one listens to kids."

"If this was Red China they would. The Red Chinese Communist Party don't play. Kids younger than that Little Girl turn their mother and father over to the Reds for treason and reeducation."

"We're not in Red China," I told her.

To that she only grunted, like "That's what you think."

Everyone Knows
the King of the Sea

I didn't care what Cecile called her new self or how much dust she blew off paths with her poems. She was Cecile Johnson to me, and I didn't appreciate her so-called new self or her new name.

A name is important. It isn't something you drop in the litter basket or on the ground. Your name is how people know you. The very mention of your name makes a picture spring to mind, whether it's a picture of clashing fists or a mighty mountain that can't be knocked down. Your name is who you are and how you're known even when you do something great or something dumb.

Cecile had no trouble dreaming up names for us. I'll bet ours were names she meant for us to keep and not throw away when we decided we had had enough of our old selves. According to Uncle Darnell and Big Ma, she had had a name ready for Fern, but Papa said, "No more of those made-up, different names." So Cecile gave Fern some of her milk, put her in her crib, stood over her for a while, and was gone.

Although no one thinks I can, I remember a time when smoke filled the house. Not coughing smoke but smoke from a woman's smooth-voiced singing, with piano, bass, and drums. All together these sounds made smoke. Uncle Darnell would say, "You can't remember that. You were two. Three, maybe." But I do. I still see, hear, and feel bits and flashes. The sounds of musical smoke. My head on Cecile's big belly. Uncle Darnell said the "Von" in "Vonetta" came from the "Vaughan" in the singer Sarah Vaughan's name. And when Uncle played the albums Cecile had left behind—the ones with piano, bass, drums, and smooth-voiced Sarah Vaughan—in my mind, smoke still filled the house.

Cecile could go changing her name at the sight of rain, but I was going to stay Delphine. Even after I learned the truth about my name. Even that wasn't enough to make me drop my name. My name was the one thing I didn't have to share with another soul in my school. In my last class, three Debras, two Lindas, two Jameses, three Michaels, and two Moniques shared their names. There was also one Anthony, whose mama could spell, and one Antnee, whose mama couldn't. It was no secret they, too, shared a name. If you hollered "Anthony," "Antnee," or "Ant," both boys' heads turned.

My name was my own, and I couldn't imagine that anyone else had it in all of Brooklyn. No matter where we went: Coney Island, Prospect Park, or Shiloh Baptist Church. There was only one Delphine.

I never thought about what Delphine meant or if it had a meaning at all. It was just my name. Delphine had a grown sound like it was waiting for me to slide into it, like a grown woman slides into a mink coat and clips on ruby earrings. I figured since Cecile didn't have a mink coat or ruby earrings to give me when I grew up, she had dreamed up a name that I would grow into. It was one thing Cecile got right. There was no slice or drop of it that I had to share with my sisters.

Then that stupid show had come on television. The one about the dolphin that saves everyone's lives and corrals the bad guys until the sheriff arrives. At recess or on the school bus, especially on Wednesdays, the day after the TV show came on, the boys would all sing, "They call him Flipper, Flipper, faster than lightning," or something like that. Then they'd start pushing at me to speak in dolphin.

Ellis Carter had been the chief Flipper singer and whistler on one particular Wednesday. I'd beaten him up real good. I'd made sure it was as unforgettable a beating as I could give him so it would burn in the minds of all the other Flipper singers and whistlers.

When I got home from school, my knuckles still sore from Ellis Carter's jaw, I'd told Vonetta and Fern to change their clothes. Hang them up neatly. That would save me from ironing them that night. I'd told them to start their homework and I'd be back in exactly twenty minutes to help them if they needed it. I'd told Big Ma I had to get a book from the library and I would be right back. Then I'd marched to that library to find out for myself. I'd gone straight to the biggest dictionary in the reference section. This was a dictionary so huge you needed both hands to manage turning the pages and making the book stay put.

Good old Merriam Webster. I trusted Merriam because I thought, instead of having children she didn't want, she wrote the dictionary. She didn't have anything else better to do, probably didn't have sisters and brothers to see after, which was why she knew every word in the world. Big Ma would have said Merriam might as well be useful.

I'd turned to the back section, turned past the Z words, past the phases of the moon and the metric system, and finally to the Given Names. I flipped a few pages to get to the female *D* names. Then I turned and thumbed past "Daisy." "Daphne." "Deanna." "Deborah." "Della.""Delores."

And there it was. The name I had been sure Cecile had dreamed up while she stared out the window as musical smoke blew through the house. There it was. In a book. Broken down into two syllables. Spelled exactly the same.

There it was. My name. Delphine.

My nostrils had flared. My breathing raced. My heart pounded not only in my chest but throughout my body.

This changed everything. My mother hadn't reached into her poetic soul and dreamt me up a name. My mother had given me a name that already was, which meant she hadn't given me a thing. Not one thing.

How could this be, when a woman's deep, smoky voice planted Vonetta's name in Cecile's mind? How could this be, when Cecile dreamed up a name for Fern so marvelous that the idea of not being able to give it caused her to up and leave us?

I didn't need to ask any further. The proof was right there. I shared my name with some other Delphine. And she, just like I, according to Miss Merriam Webster, had been named for a dolphin under the sea.

All this time I'd been holding my head up, feeling superior to Ellis, Willy, Robert, James, James, the Michaels, Anthony, and Antnee because they were stupid boys. My knuckle still smarted from socking Ellis Carter in the jaw while he had been telling the truth. I had been named for a dolphin. A big fishy mammal with a wide grin.

Learning the full truth about my name had been more than I could bear. The librarian got up from her desk and put a Kleenex in my hand. I hadn't even known I'd been making a grand Negro spectacle out of myself, bawling over a word in the dictionary.

The following week when *Flipper* came on, I'd gotten up and turned the television set off. Vonetta and Fern bleated like billy goats, but I'd done what I always did and distracted them. I'd said, "Tonight is game and cookie night." I brought out the Candy Land game, poured the milk, and piled a nice stack of Oreos on a plate. I hadn't cared if I never saw that grinning mammal again.

Coloring and La-La

The next morning, Vonetta, Fern—clutching Miss Patty Cake—and I left the green stucco house and went to the Center, where we stood on line until the doors opened for breakfast because Cecile wouldn't cook for us in her kitchen. While we ate hot oatmeal and sliced bananas, a truck from a local store pulled up and dropped off loaves of bread and crates of orange juice. Within minutes the smell of toasted bread filled the Center and small cartons of orange juice were placed on our trays.

The young white guys who delivered the bread and orange juice knew the Panthers. They stayed awhile and chatted with them. I had my eyes on them the whole time, waiting for something to happen. I felt silly once I realized all I was watching was talking and laughing. When Sister Pat came around with a basketful of toast, I grabbed two pieces, one for me and one for Fern. Vonetta, who was buddying up to one of the three sisters, could get her own toast.

It wasn't at all the way the television showed militants—that's what they called the Black Panthers. Militants, who from the newspapers were angry fist wavers with their mouths wide-open and their rifles ready for shooting. They never showed anyone like Sister Mukumbu or Sister Pat, passing out toast and teaching in classrooms.

I started to think, This place is all right. I watched the white guys leave unharmed, laughing even. I couldn't wait to tell Big Ma all about it. Then I heard Crazy Kelvin say, "That's the least that the racist dogs can do," and just like that, he spoiled what I thought I knew.

When we entered the classroom, we found the chairs and tables had been pushed to one side of the room. In the middle of the floor were white posters covered with out-lines of wavy writing. We stood on the edges of the room surrounding the posters, like we were on dry land and the posters were floating out to sea.

Sister Mukumbu motioned us in. "Sisters and brothers, find a poster to color in. You can work alone or you can work with a partner."

I looked out to sea. The letters outlined in black marker

said things like:

I had seen Huey Newton on the evening news, wearing his black beret and using his big words. Big Ma called him "the main trouble stirrer" because he was the leader of the Black Panthers. The only famous Bobby I knew was Bobby Kennedy. Even though Bobby Kennedy had been killed, I didn't think the Black Panthers wanted us to remember Bobby Kennedy. They were talking about some other Bobby. A "little" Bobby. And I wondered if he had been killed like Bobby Kennedy. Why else would they want us to remember him if he were still alive?

Sister Mukumbu said, "Yesterday we learned *revolution* means 'change' and that we can all be revolutionaries." As she spoke, we stepped carefully between the posters, choosing one and then plopping down next to it. Sister Pat passed around a bucket of Magic Markers and crayons.

Part of me felt like repeating Vonetta's words: "We didn't come for the revolution. We came for breakfast." But part of me wanted to see what it was all about. That part reached into the bucket for a thick Magic Marker. Vonetta and Fern each took crayons. Fern took an extra crayon for Miss Patty Cake.

I decided on the FREE HUEY poster since I didn't know

who Li'l Bobby was. Fern and I squatted down by our poster. Next to Fern sat Miss Patty Cake with her arms reaching out. I chose the right poster. Fern colors small and snaillike. There was no need to grab the sign with a lot of letters, since it would be just the two of us coloring. Instead of sticking with us, Vonetta ran over to the middle Ankton girl—that was their last name, Ankton—and began coloring with her and her younger sister. I couldn't say I was surprised.

Then I heard the middle Ankton girl say, "What's wrong with your little sister?"

Vonetta tried to act like she hadn't heard and kept coloring the *P* in *Power*.

"Why she run around with her dolly?"

Vonetta, who is loud and showy, showy and crowy, had to swallow her words. "She likes it. That's all." Vonetta now sounded low and small, and it served her right.

I watched Fern move her crayon in small black circles. I could hear her singing "La-la-la" to herself. I recognized the tune. It was the "la-la-la" part in a song that used to come on the radio. When Brenda and the Tabulations sang "Dry Your Eyes," my sisters and I imagined they sang about a mother who had to leave her children. It was the only real indulgence we allowed ourselves in missing having a mother. Brenda and the Tabulations, Vonetta, Fern, and I sang "Dry Your Eyes" whenever the disc jockey played it on WWRL. So I sang the la-la-la part with Fern, making a

89

nice wall around us, to keep that laughing Ankton girl on the outside.

We all have our la-la-la song. The thing we do when the world isn't singing a nice tune to us. We sing our own nice tune to drown out ugly. Fern and I colored and sang, but the middle Ankton girl was determined to break through our la-la-la wall. She had her own song and made sure we heard it.

"Your sister is a baby. Your sister is a baby."

I expected Vonetta to do what we always do. Fight back. Talk back. Pick up her crayon and scoot over near Fern and me.

Vonetta sat in a small heap of herself, looking smaller and smaller, letting that Ankton girl sing "Your sister is a baby" merrily, merrily, merrily.

I stopped filling in "Free Huey." I turned and said, "Shut up," to Vonetta's friend.

She stopped singing. That was all it took. And that made me even angrier at Vonetta. She could have done that much for her own sister.

The oldest Ankton girl rose up from her JUSTICE FOR ALL sign. She said to me, "You can't tell my sister to shut up."

I gave her a full-out neck roll. "I just did."

It didn't matter that she was almost as tall as I was, and could have been a seventh grader. It was too late to take anything back even if I wanted to.

Sister Mukumbu was right there and ended it before

90

it grew into anything to stop. She reminded us we had greater causes to fight for than to fight with each other.

"Sister Eunice, Sister Delphine. Shake hands."

We begrudgingly shook hands, then returned to our posters. I felt some shame, but I wasn't about to wear it. I was still too mad at Vonetta to be thoroughly ashamed.

On the way to Cecile's green stucco house, I said, "You're supposed to take up for Fern."

"Yeah," Fern said.

Vonetta said, "I'm tired of taking up for Fern."

Fern said, just to have something to say back, "I'm tired of taking up for you."

Vonetta said, "You don't take up for me."

"Do too."

"Do not."

"Too."

"Not."

"I do too."

"Like when?"

"When you broke the little blue teacup. I could've told."

"Big deal," Vonetta said. Then she added the Ankton girl's word to let us know who she sided with. "Big deal, baby."

Fern banged her fists at her sides and was set to leap on Vonetta, but I grabbed her in midjump. "Y'all just stop it."

Fern was near tears mad. "I'm gonna tell."

"Who you gonna tell? Cecile? She don't care about a blue teacup. Big Ma? Papa? They're miles and miles away, and we don't have enough dimes. Who you gonna tell?"

I said, "Shut up, Vonetta."

And she shut up. That was all it took.

I had planned for us to kill time playing in the park until Cecile would let us in the house, but playing in the park meant playing together. Vonetta and Fern weren't ready to play together. I had to keep my sisters apart, so instead we went to the library. Vonetta read her books at one table, and Fern and I read *Henry and Ribsy* at the next table.

When we got to Cecile's, we put our things, including Miss Patty Cake, away in our room. I asked Cecile for some money for dinner, and Fern and I went out to pick up chop suey from Ming's.

Vonetta didn't want to go, she said. And that was fine with Fern and me.

We came back from Mean Lady Ming's, who wasn't really so mean but we'd gotten used to calling her that. I kept the two dimes from the change to save up for our phone call. I was sure we'd need at least a dollar in change. Cecile wouldn't miss two dimes. If she asked for them, I'd give them to her, although I didn't think she'd ask.

We spread out the tablecloth on the floor and loaded up our plates. I said the blessing and we ate. Vonetta suddenly became Chatty Cathy all through dinner. I figured she'd had enough of being apart from Fern and me and was now glad we were all together. But it was too much Chatty Cathy for Cecile, who told Vonetta to stop disturbing the silence and that quiet was a good thing. To that Vonetta started humming that song on the radio that goes "Silence is golden, but my eyes still see." Cecile couldn't figure out how Vonetta was hers. Before Cecile did something crazy, I gave Vonetta the look and she stopped humming.

After dinner we headed for our room while Cecile put everything away. For once I didn't care that she wouldn't let us in the kitchen where her papers hung like wings. I didn't mind not having to wash dishes or mop the kitchen floor.

This was the order that we entered the room: Fern first, me next, and Vonetta last. I should have known something was amiss by the way Vonetta lagged behind. Fern and I soon learned why.

Chatty Cathy hadn't missed the company of her sisters. Chatty Cathy had been up to dirty tricks. A black Magic Marker lay on the floor. The same kind I used to color in "Free Huey."

Vonetta had gone over Miss Patty Cake with the black Magic Marker, leaving pink lips and pink rouge circles peeking out on a once-white face. To tell the truth, Miss Patty Cake was never as white as the day Fern got her. After enough biting, dragging around, and loving up, Miss Patty Cake was off-white, or "light skinned," as Fern would say. As it was, Miss Patty Cake was a long way from her pinkish white self.

Fern screamed. Louder than she'd screamed on the Coney Island Ferris wheel. Louder and longer than she'd screamed when the dentist stuck her with the novocaine needle. Fern's fists never made it to a ball. She screamed and threw her body into Vonetta like a missile flying into outer space. Vonetta and Fern fought all the time but not like this.

Cecile burst into the room and pulled them apart. That was the first time she'd touched either one of them.

She turned to me. "Why'd you let them fight like this?"

I didn't say anything. I just wanted her to come in here and act like a mother. A real one.

"Answer me, Delphine."

I raised my shoulders up and set them back down. That was my answer.

"And you, Vonetta! What do you call this?" She held up her black-scrawled grandbaby to Vonetta's face. "No wonder you couldn't stop lip flapping." To Fern she said, "You're too big for this anyway."

But Cecile still didn't offer Fern a hug. She didn't bend down and wipe Fern's tears. She still didn't call Fern by her name.

Counting and Skimming

I took a bar of Ivory soap and one of Cecile's washcloths and scrubbed away at the black ink scrawled all over Miss Patty Cake. Big Ma taught me to be a hard washboard scrubber. To not accept dirt, dust, or stains on clothes, floors, or walls, or on ourselves. "Scrub like you're a gal from a one-cow town near Prattville, Alabama," she'd tell me while Vonetta and Fern ran around and played. "Can't have you dreaming out of your head and writing on the walls. That'll only lead to ruin."

I grabbed Miss Patty Cake's dimpled arms and chubby legs. I went after her cheeks and forehead. I scrubbed every blacked-up piece of plastic, wearing down that Ivory bar from a nearly full cake to nearly half flat. I scrubbed and scrubbed until my knuckles ached. It was quite a job. When Vonetta picked up that black Magic Marker, she had been determined to make Miss Patty Cake as black and proud as Crazy Kelvin wanted her to be.

I soon found it didn't matter if I scrubbed like a gal from a one-cow town or if I gave up on Ivory soap and turned to stronger cleaners. While the heavy-duty cleaners and scouring pad lifted the black from the white bathroom sink, Miss Patty Cake's body was another story. The Magic Marker ink seeped down into Miss Patty Cake's soft plastic skin. At best, the Ajax, Pine-Sol, and scouring pad left Miss Patty Cake gray, scratched up, and strong smelling. Hard scrubbing or not, there was nothing more I could do. Miss Patty Cake would never be Fern's baby doll the way she'd been as long as anyone could remember. I shook all the water from her insides, dried her off, then put her in my suitcase to spare Fern from seeing her doll baby grayish and ashy.

I was too tired to try to make this thing between Vonetta and Fern wilt away. This wasn't exactly fighting over who gets the gold crayon or the last cookie. I knew better than to look for help from Cecile. Worn-out, I began to see things like Big Ma did. There was no point in flying us across the country for next to no mothering.

I just kept counting down the days. The best that I could do was keep Vonetta and Fern separated. Vonetta bathed by herself, and Fern bathed with me. Vonetta slept on the top of the daybed, and Fern slept with me below.

Fern no longer looked for her doll when we left Cecile's for breakfast. I wouldn't say Vonetta did Fern any favor, but maybe things worked out the way they had to.

Still, Vonetta remained proudly defiant, walking two steps ahead of us and then leaving us altogether once her new friends, the Anktons, were in sight. She and Janice, the middle Ankton, threw pebbles at Hirohito Woods and fussed over who hated him more.

For snack time, Sister Pat passed out grapes. After we ate our fill, Sister Mukumbu gave us a lesson on the California grapes that we had just eaten and how the migrant workers who picked them had to fight for their rights.

I don't think the lesson went the way Sister Mukumbu had planned. Everyone felt badly for having eaten the grapes. The room was quiet. Then Sister Mukumbu announced free time for the next hour. All the kids went wild at the prospect of running around in the park for an hour, but Fern and I didn't feel like running with them.

Sister Pat had classes at her college and had to leave. When all the kids except Fern and I ran out to the park, I asked Sister Mukumbu if she had any chores or if she needed help in the classroom. Not that I wanted her embarrassing me, having me stand up front and rotate around the sun. It just felt strange, my Timex ticking and me having nothing to do. If only I'd thought to bring my book with me. A lot of good *Island of the Blue Dolphins* did me snug inside my pillowcase.

Sister Mukumbu rose immediately. She had just the thing to keep me busy until the class came together for arts and crafts. She asked Fern and me to count the Black Panther weekly newspapers, stacking them crisscross every fifty copies. She said the older kids would take them to local stores or sell the papers themselves. She made it sound like we were doing a great service by helping the newspaper carriers become more "organized and accountable." It just gave me something to do and Fern a reason to stick with me.

Poor Fern. She didn't have the knack for counting. She was still angry and heartbroken about Miss Patty Cake. She couldn't get past twenty copies without losing her place and had to start over, again and again. My stack of papers grew while she had yet to count out her first fifty.

"Can't we just go to the park and play?" she asked.

I was tempted to let her go but said, "Come on, Fern. We have to get this done. All you have to do is count out ten and lay them this way. Then count another ten and lay them that way."

I felt Sister Mukumbu watching as I showed Fern the shortcut. You know when someone's eyes are on your back and whether it's in a good or a bad way. I felt her watching us in a good way. Soon Fern caught on, counting and crisscrossing. Her stack of papers began to grow. Not as high as mine, but it grew. Fern was now busy and not missing Miss Patty Cake for the moment.

After a short while I felt Sister Mukumbu's eyes leave us. She must have figured we were all right and had continued doing her own work.

Since the Black Panther newspaper cost a quarter, I told myself I'd only skim the front and back pages as I stacked the papers. I would read what I could see. I knew if I flipped a page over and read it line by line, I was officially reading someone else's paper. Or as Pa would call it, stealing.

I skimmed the front page of every five copies. I got into a real rhythm. Counting and reading a few key words at a time. There was more artwork than printing on the front page, so I couldn't read much. One thing was for sure. I'd know Huey Newton if I ever saw him on the street. You couldn't help but see Huey Newton all over the newspaper. His face was cocked slightly in the upper corner of the paper like the president's face on a dollar bill. Now the Black Panther leader was in prison where he belonged, according to Big Ma.

As I counted, I dug Huey's corner picture, him wearing his beret looking cool and revolutionary. I flipped open a newspaper quickly, skimmed the article in five-second glances at a time, then flipped it closed. The article was about Huey talking about Bobby. There was also a photograph of people protesting that I wanted to get a better look at. They were people carrying the same kind of signs that we had colored in. Those could have been our signs. We were probably part of the revolution. Wouldn't that make a fine classroom essay: "My Revolutionary Summer"?

I wanted to read the newspaper. Not skim. Not steal. I wanted to fold a paper over, sit back, and read every word.

I must have lost count. I was too busy imagining a Black Panther carrying our FREE HUEY sign. Too busy to notice my neat stack had grown into uneven bundles with either more than fifty or less than fifty newspapers.

"Sister Delphine."

Sister Mukumbu stood before me with a smile on her face.

"Nuts!" Fern said, because Sister Mukumbu's voice had startled her, making her lose count. She began to recount.

"Yes, Sister Mukumbu?" I answered weakly. I hadn't even heard her get up from her chair or felt her eyes on my back. It wasn't like me to get lost like that.

"Do you want to read a newspaper?"

And embarrassed. I'm not the kind to be embarrassed. Thank goodness she was a teacher and not some boy who could read the thoughts spinning in my head.

I nodded my yes, which only felt worse since I was not a nodder.

I dug out my two dimes from last night's change. "I'll

bring a nickel tomorrow," I said.

She smiled and said, "Twenty cents will be fine, Sister Delphine. You're entitled to the worker's discount."

I was too embarrassed to say thank-you and gave her another nod. I took my newspaper and folded it twice to read about Huey, Bobby, and the protesters later.

Now, instead of having two of the ten dimes needed to call Pa and Big Ma, we were back to having no dimes. Fern and I kept counting and stacking.

Big Red *S*

That night Fern complained about her aching stomach. She meowed and howled and turned in her sleep.

"Go sit on the toilet," I told her. She clung to my side, meowing and howling. Vonetta yelled, "Quit it, Fern. I can't sleep." I paid her no mind and neither did Fern. If Fern couldn't sleep, then we all couldn't sleep, so too bad for Vonetta and too bad for me. I just let Fern carry on while I rubbed her stomach. It took a while, but she finally fell into sleep.

Before we left for the Center in the morning, I asked Cecile for food money for tonight's dinner. If I could hold on to two hundred dollars over three thousand miles, I could hold on to a ten-dollar bill for a few hours. Cecile didn't bother with any questions. She just gave me the ten-dollar bill and a door key so she wouldn't have to get up and let us in. I think anyone standing at the front door made her jumpy. Even when we ate on the floor in the living room, I'd catch her eyes shift to the door when she heard a noise. Maybe she thought the Panthers were coming back to bother her for more ink and paper.

I was glad Cecile handed over the money without fuss or questions. That saved me from lying about getting shrimp lo mein when I had no intention of going to Ming's. Vonetta, Fern, and I had eaten our last plate of shrimp lo mein and egg rolls for the rest of our crazy summer. Shrimp and noodles swimming in sauce and deep-fried egg rolls had taken their toll on us. Not that Mean Lady Ming would cry for her three colored girls. She had other customers to yell at.

All day long at the Center I could think of nothing else but a home-cooked meal. We marched to the Safeway store after playing in the park for an hour. My shopping list was burned into my brain. I picked up one head of cabbage. Seventeen cents. One onion. Eight cents. Two potatoes. Twenty-three cents. One package of chicken thighs and one package of wings. One dollar and forty-seven cents. The price of the chicken would have been thievery of the highest kind, according to Big Ma, who raised chickens down in Alabama and had only to go pull one up by its neck, kill it, pluck it, clean it, and fry it. Lastly, but most important, I dropped a can of stewed prunes into our shopping basket. Forty-nine cents. There was plenty of money left over to call Pa and talk for as long as we wanted.

Vonetta and Fern pouted as the groceries went into the basket. There were even a couple of "Aw, shucks" and finger snapping as our dinner was placed on the cashier's counter. All the sniping between Vonetta and Fern over Miss Patty Cake was now aimed at their new enemies: the real food that we would eat until we returned to Brooklyn, and me.

I paid for the groceries and put the change in my pocket. I'd give Cecile the dollar bills and keep the coins for our telephone call to Papa.

"Why can't we have pizza?" Vonetta moaned.

"Or shrimp lo mein?"

"Because," I said, enjoying my role as their enemy and big sister, "that's not food for everyday eating." I held up the brown paper Safeway bag with its big red *S* printed smack in the center. "This is."

Big Ma would have been proud of me but also angry that I allowed it to come to this. I'm sure she expected this kind of living from Cecile. From me she expected better.

"Phooey."

"Double phooey."

They could phooey all night long for all I cared.

Vonetta said, "I hope you know she won't let you cook that."

"Not in her kitchen," Fern said.

So I said, "Then she'll cook it in her kitchen." Papa's voice poured out of my mouth like warm, steady tap water.

When I put the key in the door, I said, "Go wash your face and hands real good. Play Go Fish until I call you for supper."

Cecile wasn't in the living room, which meant she was in her kitchen. I didn't want Vonetta and Fern to see how afraid I was of Cecile. I thought of how she planted her body between us and her kitchen door, daring us to take a step farther. That she'd rather let Fern dry up of thirst than give her a glass of water with ice. I thought about how crazy Cecile was and that I didn't know her or what she would do next.

Now that I could smell the cabbage and onion from the brown paper bag, I lost that feeling of being calm and brave like Papa. I didn't dare walk in, so I called to her: "Cecile."

It didn't occur to me to use her poet name, Nzila, to maybe soften her up. But that name didn't feel right coming out of my mouth.

I dreaded this moment. Dreaded the thought of her swinging the kitchen door open and her seeing me with a bag of uncooked food. There was no putting it off. I called to her again, this time louder: "Cecile."

Her hands slapped against the counter or tabletop good

and hard. In a few stomps the door swung open and she was looking down at me.

I took a step back and hugged the bag. "I have to cook supper."

She stared down at me and didn't speak. I didn't know what to do or say, so I took the change out of my pocket, all of it, and held it out to her. She took it. Dropped it into her pants pocket. Maintained her long, hard stare. If that was supposed to make me feel afraid, stupid, and small, it worked.

Then she spoke. "Whyn't you go to Ming's? Or Shabazz?"

We have a Shabazz in Brooklyn. The fish and bean pie place run by the Black Muslims.

I found my voice and said, "We can't eat takeout every day. Vonetta and Fern can't stomach it."

"You can't come in my kitchen making a mess. This is my workplace. I don't need you in here turning things upside down."

I said, "I don't make messes," without a lick of sass. I spoke the plain truth. I'd never made a mess in my life. Not even for the fun of it.

Cecile went stomping and cursing back into the kitchen. "No one told y'all to come out here. No one wants you out here making a mess, stopping my work."

I stood outside the kitchen with the Safeway bag held tight to my chest. I'm sure the Safeway *S* was in the same spot as Superman's big red *S* was sewn to his costume. I felt right about looking out for my sisters, but I didn't feel brave. All the same, I didn't want Vonetta and Fern to see me standing there like a scared dummy holding a bag of groceries.

Cecile pushed the door open.

"Get a speck of grease on my work . . . You hear?"

I knew better than to wait for a nicer invitation and walked inside Cecile's kitchen. It was larger than our kitchen back home. Hers had both the cooking area and an eating area, which hadn't been set up for eating. There was a long table, only one chair—hers—and what I figured was her printing machine on top of the table.

I didn't want to be caught gawking at her and her stuff. I went straight to the sink and started stripping the onion. Washing the cabbage. Washing potatoes. Washing the chicken parts until I could figure out what to do next without having to ask Cecile a thing.

She hovered over her machinery, grunting and cursing. Then she got up, pulled open a drawer, and threw a potato peeler and a knife in the sink. The knife just missed my hand. She didn't look once but said, "Don't go cutting off your fingers. There's no money to take you to the hospital."

I felt her watching me at work. Thanks to Big Ma, I could skin a potato with a paring knife without wasting a scrap of white potato. I could cut up a whole fryer too, even though this time I didn't have to.

Cecile grunted. "What you gonna do to that chicken?"

I said, "Bake it."

"Frying's faster," she said.

I pointed to her papers. "Grease." Papa's easy voice just slid right out of me, warm and steady. I could feel myself coming back. My voice. My steadiness.

"What you gonna do with the potatoes?"

"Boil them with the cabbage and onion."

"Hmp."

There was something about being here with her in the kitchen. And I knew what it was. I had a flash. A flash of us. Quiet and in the kitchen. Pencil tapping and her voice chanting. I blinked that flash away. I didn't have time to be pulled into a daydream. I kept doing what I was doing. And then I pressed my luck and asked her for some fatback.

Another grunt. "No fatback. No salt pork. No pig of any kind in my kitchen."

I shook my head. People in Oakland were touchy about pigs. They were touchy about the pig on their plates and the "pigs," as Crazy Kelvin called them, in police cars. Back in Brooklyn, Big Ma wouldn't stand for cooking without pork on a Sunday. I couldn't even imagine Cecile and Big Ma sharing a kitchen or living in the same house.

Since there was no pork, I used what Cecile had. Butter, salt and pepper, plus the onion. It didn't smell like

Big Ma's kitchen in Brooklyn, but it was the aroma of real food cooking.

Now that I had our dinner under way, I wanted to take in Cecile's place of work. See what she was doing hovering over her machine, quietly. Carefully. From where I stood, stealing glances, it seemed like she was laying down puzzle pieces. Picking up one piece of something and laying it carefully down on her equipment. Picking up another piece and laying it down. Then she'd study the pieces. Just the piece she had completed. She had pulled herself into her puzzle laying and had forgotten I was there.

I could see why Vonetta and Fern were not allowed inside Cecile's kitchen. Cecile was fixed in prayer. I was allowed to be there, but I didn't dare clear my throat, let alone ask her to show me what she was doing. Vonetta and Fern didn't have the sense to be quiet.

We spread the tablecloth on the floor and sat cross-legged as if we were eating Mean Lady Ming's takeout or fried fish from Shabazz. While Vonetta and Fern ate begrudgingly, Cecile cleaned her plate and left three blanched chicken bones.

"This don't taste like Big Ma's," Vonetta said.

"Surely don't," Fern followed.

"We shoulda got pizza."

"Or shrimp lo mein."

Cecile reached onto Vonetta's plate and took the thigh

that Vonetta had left. To me, she said, "That's gratitude for you."

I didn't care that they were ungrateful. I told my sisters, "Get used to eating like this."

Vonetta said, "I'm going to tell Big Ma."

"And Papa."

To them, I said, "Tell."

When we were done, Cecile handed me every plate, after she'd eaten whatever Vonetta and Fern had left. "You started this mess, Delphine. You clean every dish and spoon."

We had eaten with forks, but I wasn't about to correct her. I just took the forks while Vonetta and Fern disappeared into our room. At least I could look Pa in the eye and say, "Yes, Pa. I did what you said. I looked out for my sisters." At least I got Cecile to let me into her kitchen.

Then she added, "And don't expect no help from me."

I said, "I don't mind."

She gave another *"Hmp"* and a headshake. "We're trying to break yokes. You're trying to make one for yourself. If you knew what I know, seen what I've seen, you wouldn't be so quick to pull the plow."

I sort of knew what she meant, but someone had to look out for Vonetta and Fern while we were here.

I stacked the plates in the sink and ran the hot water.

"It wouldn't kill you to be selfish, Delphine," she said, and moved me out of the way to wash her hands. Then she went back to praying over her puzzle pieces.

China Who

Sister Mukumbu gave Eunice, Hirohito, and me two empty milk cartons each to fill with water from the hallway fountain. Today our class was to take sponges that she and Sister Pat had cut up into different shapes and make printed designs on old T-shirts. We'd use red, black, and green paint, the same colors as the ink Cecile used for her poems and whatever flyers the Panthers asked her to print up.

As Sister Mukumbu readied the paints, I thought of all those colors, dripping and splattering on Vonetta's and Fern's clothes, and having to scrub them without a washboard.

"Don't start anything until I get back with the water," I told Fern.

Fern seemed off in a world of her own.

Sister Mukumbu clapped her hands, pressing me to get going. Fern would be all right for two minutes without me.

I followed Eunice and Hirohito with a mind to hurry back. I had to admit, I liked being seen as one of the classroom helpers. Vonetta and Janice were put out by the fact that they weren't asked to take a skip down the hall with Hirohito. They had both raised their hands to ask if they could help too. Although I didn't like Eunice much, we glanced at each other and knew the same thing: our middle sisters were boy crazy for Hirohito. He was probably twelve or thirteen and only saw Vonetta and Janice as pests he could both mess with and keep at a distance.

Hirohito beat us to the fountain. As he filled up his cartons, I studied every feature of his face. I wanted to ask him how it felt to have slanted eyes, hair like pine needles, and coppery-colored skin. Which one was he more: Chinese or colored? If I were Vonetta, I would have at least asked him that, as much as she's always in his face. I would have asked him something interesting instead of "Do you like short girls or tall girls?"

I knew my curiosity didn't excuse my staring or wanting to pry. After all, I certainly didn't like questions about not having a mother. So I scolded myself good, while Hirohito filled up his second carton: I should keep my curiosity to myself; I should not stare at his long black eyelashes and

coppery-colored skin. Besides, I couldn't go from plan-
ning to sock him to asking him about being a colored
Chinese boy in one good blink. But before I had a chance
to look away, he caught me staring at him.

"What?"

I gave it back. "Did I say something to you?" Thank
goodness you can't see cherries in a chocolate bar. I'd
have been a red-faced rose if not for my Hershey brown
complexion.

"Take a picture. It lasts longer."

"I was not looking at you, boy." Girl pride made me lie
hard and strong.

Eunice gave me a "Were too" glare, but I couldn't let
this boy think I was staring at him even if he caught me
red-faced beneath my brown skin. I couldn't let this boy
with slanted eyes and copper-colored skin think I thought
a thing about him. Because I didn't.

"And if you try to run me and my sisters off the sidewalk
with that skateboard, I'm going to stomp on you good."

We were about the same height, but I hadn't met a boy
I couldn't throw down to the ground. But then, I was taller
than all the boys I knew.

"I yelled for you to get out of the way. Can I help it if
you're slow?" He was no Ellis Carter, Anthony, Antnee, or
the other boys who tapped me from behind and ran. He
spoke calmly, with no fear of my boy-throwing abilities.

"Well, you shouldn't be skateboarding where people walk."

113

"Girl, that's no skateboard," he said, full of what I guessed was boy pride. "That's my go-kart."

"Who cares, China boy."

He gave me a look like he was going to drop both cartons and put up his dukes. One eyebrow went up. "China who?"

I was glad he said that because my "China you" shot out right on time.

Eunice jumped in and said, "For your information, he's black and Japanese. Can't you tell the difference between a Japanese name and a Chinese name?"

I didn't like having my ignorance shoved at me, especially by the likes of Eunice Ankton. But there I was. Not knowing a half-Chinese face from a half-Japanese one. I wasn't about to get a better look so I'd know the difference. Looking at that stupid boy got me red-faced in the first place. The last thing I'd do was own up to my ignorance and then apologize.

I turned to Eunice as if Hirohito weren't there. "I don't care what he is. He just better watch out when he's riding that skateboard on the sidewalk."

Hirohito turned and started walking back to the classroom. "Go-kart."

I said, "Forget you, Hirohito."

He said, "Forgot you, Delphine."

Then I said quickly to get the last lick, "Never thought about you."

Eunice said, "Is that what you all say where you come from? That's so corny."

For Eunice's information, there was more to that rhyme. *Swallow a snake, jump in the lake, come back home with a bellyache.* It did sound corny, so I kept it to myself. "I don't care."

She walked ahead of me. "If you knew about Hirohito and Brother Woods, you'd leave him alone."

Then I got suckered into a school-yard comeback I should have seen coming. "What about Hirohito and Brother Woods?"

Wouldn't you know it? Eunice had hips. She made sure I knew that fact as she walked ahead of me. "That's for me to know and for you to find out."

Expert
Colored Counting

Vonetta and Fern figured that since I talked my way inside Cecile's kitchen, I should fight harder for other things, namely to have a television set in the house. It was bad enough knowing our California vacation wasn't much to hang a back-to-school essay on. There were no Disneyland rides to write about. No Hollywood movie stars in the Safeway store to sign autographs. No surfing at the beach or shaking peaches or plums from fruit trees in the back-yard. There wasn't even a long-lost mama hugging and crying at the airport.

I soon saw my sisters' point. The least we could have was a television set. Cartoons on Saturdays, funny shows after dinner, the evening news and true-crime shows for me. And of course, *The Mike Douglas Show* five days a week because Mike Douglas always had Negro performers on his variety show. Outside of the Flipper incident, we didn't fight over TV, which would mean less noise to bother Cecile. If she bought a portable TV set, we could put it in our room and she wouldn't have to see us for hours. Then it would feel like a real vacation. Watching hours and hours of *Get Smart* and *The F.B.I.* without Big Ma making us turn the set off.

Once again I found my calm, steady voice and brought our demands to Cecile at our next sit-down dinner. That's what protesters did. They brought their protest songs and their demands to the Establishment, because the Establishment was in control. The Establishment was someone over thirty years old who had the power. I didn't know Cecile's exact age, but she had to be over thirty. That, plus her holding on to the money Pa had given us, had made Cecile the Establishment. All we needed were some protest signs and an "or else" that wouldn't make Cecile mad enough to hurt us. Without an "or else," protesters are just people with protest songs and demands who don't stand a chance of getting anything. The only things Cecile seemed to care about were her poems and her peace and quiet. The only thing we seemed to care about was our television set. Armed with that, I brought up our sole demand and stood ready with our reasons, as if my Safeway *S* were pressed to my chest.

She said, "No one *needs* a television set."

"We do," I said.

"To catch our shows," Vonetta said.

"Yeah," Fern said. "To catch our cartoons."

"And the evening news," I threw in. You could practically see the whole world on the evening news.

"And Mike Douglas."

"That's right. We want Mike Douglas."

How else would we see Motown groups, James Brown, or Aretha Franklin?

The Mike Douglas Show wasn't the only place to find colored people on television. Each week, *Jet* magazine pointed out all the shows with colored people. My sisters and I became expert colored counters. We had it down to a science. Not only did we count how many colored people were on TV, we also counted the number of words the actors were given to say. For instance, it was easy to count the number of words the Negro engineer on *Mission Impossible* spoke as well as the black POW on *Hogan's Heroes*. Sometimes the black POW didn't have any words to say, so we scored him a "1" for being there. We counted how many times Lieutenant Uhuru hailed the frequency on *Star Trek*. We'd even take turns being her, although Big Ma would have never let us wear a minidress or space boots. But then there was *I Spy*. All three of us together couldn't count every word Bill Cosby said. And then there was a new show, *Julia*, coming in September, starring Diahann Carroll. We agreed to shout out "Black Infinity!" when *Julia* came on because each episode would be all about her character.

We didn't just count the shows. We counted the commercials as well. We'd run into the TV room in time to catch the commercials with colored people using deodorant, shaving cream, and wash powder. There was a little colored girl on our favorite commercial who looked just like Fern. In fact, I said that little girl could have been Fern, which made Vonetta jealous. In the commercial, the little girl took a bite of buttered bread and said, "Gee, Ma. This is the best butter I ever ate." Then we'd say it the way she did, in her dead, expressionless voice; and we'd outdo ourselves trying to say it with the right amount of deadness. We figured that that was how the commercial people told her to say it. Not too colored. Then we'd get silly and say it every kind of colored way we knew how.

We gave Cecile all of our reasons why she should have a television set in her green stucco house. We even showed her how it would give her peace of mind to do her work without us bothering her. To our reasons, the Establishment said, "Television is a liar and a story." But we weren't ready to give up.

"The evening news comes on television," I said. "That's all true because it's on the news."

She grunted.

"And the weatherman gives the weather report. That's important."

Another grunt.

"And the Monkees do the monkey." Then Fern swung her arms up and down and bopped her head like a go-go dancer.

Cecile made a "what" expression. Flummoxed. Good old Fern! Fern had managed to completely flummox the Establishment.

And then we started singing our protest song, chewing away at her peace and quiet: "Here we come. Walking down the street. . . ." like Davy Jones, Micky Dolenz, and the other singing Monkees.

The next day when we came back from the Center, we found a radio in our room, the cord wrapped around its plastic body. It was a sho-'nuf, left-by-the-garbage-dump, secondhand radio. Vonetta and Fern squealed as if the little colored girl in the commercial were standing in our room eating buttered bread.

Civic Pride

We'd been learning about civics since the first grade. There was always a field trip to the fire station on Henry Street. We watched the same film about the firemen, policemen, and mayor, who kept our community safe and orderly. The film's narrator reminded every boy—from Ellis Carter to the Jameses, the Anthonys, and every other pants wearer—that they too could grow up to be guardians of our community. We girls were reminded that we could look forward to becoming teachers, nurses, wives, and mothers. Poets were never mentioned.

At the Center we had a civics lesson. We were being taught our rights as citizens and how to protect those rights when dealing with the police. Sister Mukumbu used the word "policeman," while Crazy Kelvin, who filled in for Sister Pat, preferred to say "the racist pig." He broke our rights down step-by-step as if there was no time to lose. Any given day a police car could stop my sisters and me on our way from the Safeway market and search our bag of groceries. We had to be armed with our rights.

As the lesson went on, it seemed like all Crazy Kelvin wanted was to get us to call the police "the pigs." He started with Hirohito. "My man, Hirohito, who knocked down your door and arrested your father?"

Hirohito's face fell to the table. He looked worse than when Sister Mukumbu asked him to revolve and spin around the sun. He picked at a flaky piece of skin on his thumb. Normally I'd think, Ew, nasty boy. How disgusting. Instead I felt sorry for him with Crazy Kelvin poking at him.

Hirohito answered, "The police."

Crazy Kelvin said, "The who?"

Hirohito said, "The Oakland police."

That wasn't good enough for Crazy Kelvin, whom we had to call Brother Kelvin in the classroom. He looked like a bony, big-beaked chicken going "The who? The who?" It was like the time he shouted "black girl" at my sisters and me, while we shouted back "colored girl."

It didn't take sharp eyes to see Sister Mukumbu was annoyed with her helper and as usual, stepped in to put an end to it. Crazy Kelvin was supposed to talk to us about our rights, not to stand there going "The who? The who?"

Big-beaked Crazy Kelvin wasn't done. He said, "The pigs broke down the door of a Vietnam war hero's house. The pigs handcuffed him without respect for his rights as a citizen. The racist pigs then separated Brother Woods from his family because he dared speak the truth to the people."

Hirohito tried to show no change in his face, but he was changing on the inside, where people change when they're sad or angry. He looked directly at me, then looked away. I felt like I was supposed to say something to him, but I didn't know what.

Sister Mukumbu thanked Brother Kelvin for being our guest speaker and showed him to the door.

Fern tugged the hem of my top. "I don't like him. Surely don't."

I glanced Eunice Ankton's way. I had just found out what she had meant when we were out by the water fountain. That Hirohito's father was in prison for speaking out to the people. Hirohito's father was what Sister Mukumbu called a "freedom fighter" and a "political prisoner." Although, now that I knew, I didn't find any satisfaction in having found out.

Imagine. To have your father sitting down eating dinner or shining his shoes while watching TV. To have your front door blown off its hinges and the police rush in. To see your father in handcuffs, led away.

Hirohito didn't have to imagine. He knew.

I had been scared once. Truly scared for Papa. It happened two summers ago. Big Ma had gone back to Alabama ahead of us to visit family and take care of her house. We had packed up the Wildcat and had driven down to Alabama so my sisters and I could stay there for the summer. We had been driving all day, all night. Talk about being a long way from home. If we needed to stop, we found a gas station or a nice colored family to open their home to us. As we drove deeper south, down dark highways and even darker back roads, I felt like Dorothy in *The Wizard of Oz*. I told myself, "Delphine, we are no longer in Brooklyn."

Papa had pulled the car off the road so we could catch a few hours of sleep. I remember Vonetta snoring on one side of me, Fern with Miss Patty Cake burrowed into my side. Somehow I managed to find myself snoring with my sisters and Papa. Then there had been a loud rap against the window. Balls of flashlight ghosts had flown all around the back- and front seats, all over our faces. It had been a state policeman. Papa had rolled down his window and shown the state policeman his license and said he was driving his girls down to see their grandma in Alabama. The state policeman hadn't offered directions. He hadn't called Papa "Mr. Gaither, sir," or "citizen" like the helpful police officer in our civic-pride film. I heard what that state policeman called Papa. I heard it all right. I held on to Fern tight, afraid for Papa. Afraid Papa might talk back or fight back.

When we had arrived at Big Ma's, I'd expected that Pa would have told Big Ma all about it. How we couldn't stop and pee anywhere we wanted to. How the state police had rapped on the window. What he'd called Papa. How Papa hadn't hauled back like Cassius Clay and socked the policeman's jaw into the next county. Papa could tell some stories. He speaks them so plain, you believe every word. I knew Papa would have entertained Big Ma.

When Big Ma asked, "How'd the trip go?" Pa had said, "We made it down sure 'nuf. You know, Ma. Same old same old."

Rally for Bobby

When Sister Pat pinned the picture of Bobby Hutton to the wall next to the other revolutionaries I learned who he was. I finally read about him in the Black Panther newspaper. The article reported how the people wanted to name the park after Bobby. The article also retold what had happened to him. I kind of remembered having watched the news with Big Ma a few months ago and hearing about the shooting in Oakland. Now the shooting seemed closer. More real.

Bobby Hutton was the first member of the Black Panthers, other than the leaders. He was so young, the Black Panther leaders—Huey Newton and Bobby Seale—made him get his mother's permission to join. He was also the youngest Black Panther to die for the cause. He was only six years older than I was.

The newspaper had said how the police ambushed the Black Panthers while they were in a car and how the Panthers fled inside a house for shelter. That there was a shoot-out. That the police fired at the Panthers and the Panthers fired at the police. That when Little Bobby came outside to surrender, and took off all his clothes except for his underwear to show he had no gun, they shot him anyway. Over and over and over. That was this past April. Two days after Reverend King was killed.

After reading about Bobby Hutton, I had begun to look around at the Panthers who helped out at the Center. And the young ones on the streets, patrolling or passing by. I had looked real hard at them and had seen that they were teenagers or were a little older, like Sister Pat and Crazy Kelvin. I couldn't stand Crazy Kelvin, never called him Brother Kelvin or went out of my way to speak to him. But I didn't want to see him get shot because he was wearing his OFF THE PIG T-shirt.

Reading that article had made me both angry and afraid. Angry someone as young as Bobby had been killed and afraid that if he could get shot for being with the Panthers, maybe it was too dangerous for us to be at the Black Panthers' summer camp. After all, they weren't teaching us how to deal with the police for nothing. And I was tall for my age. No one would think I was just a girl going on twelve. The police who patrolled the Center could be chasing someone, burst in, shoot first, and ask questions later.

Maybe we didn't have to come to the Center to learn our rights and to have breakfast. If Cecile let me cook dinner in her kitchen, she'd let me fry some eggs or pour some cereal in her kitchen too. Being in Cecile's house might have been crazy. Her house might not have been smothered with love. But being in Cecile's house was at the very least safe. We were better off in that green stucco house with Cecile.

What would Papa have said if he knew I was bringing Vonetta and Fern to a summer school where police cars drove by to see what we were doing? I was supposed to look after Vonetta and Fern, not put them in danger.

I wished I hadn't opened up that newspaper. I wished I could go right on thinking we were having breakfast, painting signs, and learning our rights. I wished I didn't know that I was marching my sisters into a boiling pot of trouble cooking in Oakland. But it was too late for wishing. I knew full well what I knew.

I could barely give Sister Mukumbu my full attention. She said we would be attending a rally two Saturdays from today. Something about freeing Huey and naming the park across the street after Little Bobby Hutton. Hearing Bobby Hutton's name had shaken me out of my thoughts. My hand shot up before I had words formed in my mind. I knew "rally" meant "protest" and that "protest" could mean "riot." After all, I read the papers. I watch the evening news. A protest was never a love-in.

Sister Mukumbu was still smiling when she recognized me. I bet she thought I was going to talk about the newspaper article or say something revolutionary. I said, "I'm sorry, Sister Mukumbu. But my sisters and I can't go to the rally." I knew I surprised her because I'm not an "I can't" kind of person. I might as well have said, "We didn't come here for the revolution."

Sister Pat said, "Don't worry, Sis. I know Sister Nzila. She'll let you go."

I got over her saying she knew my mother when I barely knew Cecile. Besides, I had bigger fish to fry. I said, "It's not my mother who's saying no. *I'm* saying no. We can't go."

Then Vonetta called out, "We can too go to the rally."

And Fern said, "We surely can."

Vonetta and Fern didn't know what they were saying. They just didn't want to be left out of any activity concerning those Ankton girls or that Hirohito, still wearing his same old Oakland Raiders jersey.

Sister Mukumbu asked for respect and order in the classroom. We quieted down. She said she would speak to me later and continued talking about the rally and honoring Bobby Hutton and freeing Huey. Then she said the very thing that was sure to defeat me. She said, "We have been asked to do a special presentation at the rally."

My sisters' faces lit up.

"We could perform a play, do a group dance, or recite poetry. Or if anyone has a special talent to display, you can do that too."

I was sunk. "Talent to display" was enough to sway Vonetta and Fern. There was no way to keep Vonetta from throwing herself onstage after Sister Mukumbu said those three words.

Vonetta is all ham and show. Any occasion, even a riot in the making, would have been good enough to perform at. Fern is no better. She sings like a bird, is cute, and, like Vonetta, cannot resist the lure of applause and attention.

I don't have anything to be vain about. I have no talent to show. Even if I did, I have no desire to throw myself before people for their applause. I dance because the lessons are paid for and Papa feels all girls should dance ballet and tap. I sing in the children's choir because Big Ma makes sure we motherless girls enjoy all the pitying looks the church can spare, whether we want them or not.

Later, during free time, Hirohito and the boys started doing karate and jujitsu moves. The Ankton girls huddled to talk about what they would do for their special talent. From the looks of their gesturing, they would dance an African dance. The other kids just played. I expected Vonetta to run off and join the Anktons. But Vonetta told Fern and me, "We should sing a song."

Fern added, "We should sing a song and do a dance."

Before I could say why we shouldn't, they started.

"We can wave our arms pretty like the Supremes."

"And wear our hair like the Supremes."

"Or wild like Tina Turner."

"And the Ikettes."

"Ooh! Ooh! We can sing our song," Vonetta said.

"Yeah. Our song," Fern said.

I pretended I didn't know which song they meant, but I knew. Just to make sure I knew, Vonetta and Fern sang the first three words to "Dry Your Eyes" on cue.

"No," I said.

They sang louder. Fern's voice sweet and high, Vonetta's drippy and dramatic.

"No," I told them. "We're not singing that."

They ignored me and belted out the heartbreaker part where the mother must leave her baby. Then they sang the la-la parts.

By now everyone looked our way, so I hushed Vonetta and Fern, whose eyes shone with life and sparkle. I had no hope of reeling either back to their good common sense.

"We are not singing that song," I said plainly. To their "Why not?" pouting faces I said, "This presentation is for the people. For Bobby Hutton and Huey Newton. It's not for singing about your broken heart to your long-lost mother."

But they insisted on Brenda and the Tabulations. They insisted on letting the world in on their longing for a

131

mother who wouldn't cook a meal for them.

I put my foot down. "We cannot sing that song."

"Can too," they started.

Vonetta said, "And then she'll come to the talent show and see us onstage."

"And see how good we are."

It didn't seem right that they thought singing and dancing would change Cecile into someone who cried for her long-lost daughters or fried pork chops and made banana pudding. Cecile wasn't that kind of mother, if you wanted to call her one at all. Her name might have changed. She might have been living on the other side of the country. But Cecile was plain old Cecile. Just crazier and scarier than I remembered.

I told them outright, "We could sing 'Dry Your Eyes' like Brenda and the Tabulations and dance like the Ikettes. Cecile won't come to the rally and cheer us on."

They said I was wrong about Cecile and wrong about what we could and could not sing for the talent show.

I said, "Those people aren't rallying for a TV set. They're rallying to free Huey and to change the name of the park. The mayor, the judge, and the police aren't going to just say, 'Fine by us.' There's going to be trouble cooking at the rally."

Vonetta sang, "Spoilsport. Worrywart." Then Fern joined her.

I said, "Fine. But I'm not singing with you."

Sister Mukumbu said she needed help with something. Everyone raised his or her hand, but she called my name even though I kept my hand down. I couldn't say I was surprised.

Sister Mukumbu said, "What's troubling you, Sister Delphine? Why don't you want to participate in the rally?"

"Sister Mukumbu, it's all dangerous. Just being here at the Center is dangerous."

She was silent for a while. "I see." That meant she wasn't going to lie to me. I wanted to still like her. I couldn't if she lied to me.

"I have to look out for my sisters, you know."

Sister Mukumbu said, "We look out for each other. The rally is one way of looking out for all of our sisters. All of our brothers. Unity, Sister Delphine. We have to stand united."

I was thinking, Alive. We have to be alive. Wouldn't Little Bobby rather be alive than be remembered? Wouldn't he rather be sitting out in the park than have the park named after him? I wanted to watch the news. Not be in it. The more I thought about it, the more I had my answer. We were staying home tomorrow and the next day and the day after that. We certainly weren't going to be in no rally.

Eating Crow

The next morning, Cecile stood outside our door and said, "It's nine o'clock. Why y'all still here?"

Vonetta pointed to me. "It's her fault."

Fern joined in. "All her fault."

"She won't take us to the Center."

"Yeah. She said we can't go no more."

Cecile turned to me. "Delphine, what did you do?"

I spoke as plainly as I could. There was no use in speaking small mouthed. "I told Sister Mukumbu we're not going to the Free Huey rally two Saturdays from now, or coming back to the Center."

"Why'd you tell her that?"

"It's dangerous," I said. "The police shot a teenager for

being with the Black Panthers. They could shoot Black Panthers and kids at the Center."

Cecile looked at me like I was stupid, but also with disbelief that I was her daughter. "Did anyone shoot at you, Delphine?" Her voice was calm and clear. Not crazy.

I felt stupid. "No."

"Did they point a gun at you?"

"No."

"Did anyone put a gun in your hand?"

"No."

Cecile said, "Y'all get dressed and go. They might still be serving breakfast."

I couldn't believe she'd make us go back to a place where we could get shot. But then I returned to my good common sense. Of course Cecile wouldn't care if we got shot up by the police.

I told Cecile, "We'll go for breakfast. We'll go for summer school. We won't be going to no rally. That's just a pot of boiling trouble cookin'."

"Y'all two. Get in there and brush your teeth. Wash your faces." Cecile crooked her head toward the bathroom. As soon as Vonetta and Fern got up and left the room, she stepped in closer to me. I was genuinely afraid.

"You watch how you talk to me. Y'hear?"

I nodded in reply, and I was no nodder.

She wouldn't accept my nod. "No," she said. "You got a mouth, so I want to hear you."

I said, "Yes, ma'am." That old-fashioned word just crawled right out.

Cecile grunted. "That's the problem right there. His mammy. You sound just like her. Like a country mule." I think that set Cecile off more than my saying we weren't going to the rally. Me sounding like Big Ma.

Cecile went back to her kitchen, fussing up a full steam like she was talking to someone. Me. That she couldn't have us here messing up her peace of mind and that she couldn't work with us in her house. Cecile carried on a full conversation, on and on as we walked out the door. Crazy.

Vonetta and Fern were only too glad to be headed toward the Center. They couldn't stop rubbing it in.

"See, Delphine, you can't tell us what to do," Vonetta said.

"Surely can't."

" 'Cause we're going to the Center, and we're going to the rally."

"Surely are."

"And we're going to sing our song."

"And do our dance."

"And you can't be in it with us."

But Fern didn't go along with Vonetta on the last one, not that I wanted to be in it. Still, a small part of me was glad. Fern had always been mine.

* * *

I wasn't in a hurry to go inside when we got to the Center, but I followed my sisters when they pushed the doors open. Vonetta and Fern couldn't eat the late breakfast and rejoin Sister Mukumbu's class fast enough. I found myself dragging behind them, feeling badly for myself. No one ever called a take-back "eating crispy fried chicken." They called it "eating crow," and with good reason. Not that I'd actually eaten a black crow, but with my words stuck in my throat and my eyes cast down, I knew what eating crow was. I knew that having to eat crow when you were once proud and right was like swallowing a hunk of tough, chewy crow meat that wasn't about to go down easy.

Sister Mukumbu didn't make me feel like the nothing I knew I was. Her bangles jangled about her wrists as she welcomed us back into class. Everyone was practicing their parts in a play for the rally, and she said we had arrived just in time. They could use more actors for the class's reenactment of Harriet Tubman leading slaves to freedom. Vonetta was mad because Janice was to be Harriet Tubman. I knew I'd hear about Vonetta missing out on being the star of the play for the next seven days.

Later, after Sister Pat led us through calisthenics in the yard, Eunice came over and sat with me. "Thought ya'll weren't coming back."

"We weren't."

"Then why're you here?"

Eunice had a lot of nerve and a lot of mouth, asking me

why my sisters and I were back at the Center. I had noth-ing to say to Eunice. I already felt bad.

I shrugged, although I was no shrugger.

"You were just showing off, telling Sister Mukumbu how you and your sisters weren't coming to the rally, like you're in charge."

"For your information, I am in charge of my sisters."

"Oh yeah? So why are you back, then?"

The last thing I would do was tell Eunice Ankton that we were here because Cecile shooed us away to write her poems.

" 'Cause," I said.

I couldn't figure out why Eunice sat there with me. It was bad enough to feel stupid. I didn't need anyone sitting with me reminding me of it.

My sisters were having a good time. Fern and the young-est Ankton girl, Beatrice, taught each other hand-clapping songs. Janice and Vonetta chased after Hirohito and his friends, but they were only after Hirohito. He'd zig left and right, escaping the girls each time they came within tag-ging distance. Finally Janice managed to tag him and run. Vonetta was upset that she hadn't tagged him first, but that didn't stop her from cackling and squealing along with Jan-ice. Janice and Vonetta were one and the same fool.

Eunice beat me to making a sound of disgust.

I said, "I wouldn't hardly be chasing after no Hirohito Woods."

"Me neither," she agreed.

I hated telling her I was only going into the sixth grade when she was going into the eighth grade. At least I was an inch taller than she was. Hirohito, she said, was going into the seventh grade.

I told Eunice her dress was nice. Then she showed me the inside stitching. Once I saw the crisscross of her mother's neat hand stitching I decided I liked Eunice Ankton. She wasn't the big girl who thought her clothes were better than mine. Or the girl who sided with Hirohito Woods and made me feel ignorant for not knowing he was half colored and half Japanese. We were two older sisters watching our younger sisters playing games and running around making fools of themselves. We were both the oldest girls in our families, and we knew the same things.

Itsy Bitsy Spider

Vonetta couldn't stop practicing her poem. Well, it wasn't hers. She got it from a book of Negro poets at the Center. If she couldn't sing her song, she would recite a poem all by herself.

It wasn't enough for Vonetta to say her poem, which was actually Gwendolyn Brooks's poem titled "We Real Cool." Vonetta tried to *be* her poem. Since there was no applause from Fern and me the first time around, she started up again, as zombielike as she could, to imitate the toughs standing around outside the pool hall. If Big Ma heard Vonetta and saw her standing like a shiftless bum on the corner, we'd be on the next plane back to New York City. Vonetta was into a groove and couldn't be stopped. She started up yet again, saying every line of "We Real Cool" as loud as she could, in case Cecile hadn't heard her. I would have done both Vonetta and Cecile a favor by giving her a swift kick, but I didn't care if Cecile yelled at her. I didn't care if Vonetta disturbed Cecile's peace of mind. So I let Vonetta recite "We Real Cool" on and on.

Vonetta was a perfectionist, but only about certain things. Things that would get her noticed or earn her applause. Big Ma said Vonetta wouldn't be such a show-off if Cecile had picked Vonetta up more when she was a baby hollering in her crib. I didn't need a flash of memory to recall Vonetta's crying. She cried loudly and a lot.

Our door was open and Cecile was in the living room, lying on her beat-up sofa. Cecile could hear Vonetta perfectly well. Vonetta had said this poem seven times so far. I was certain her aim was to say it ten times each night, but Cecile didn't let her get that far. It took only six angry foot stomps for Cecile to make it back to our room.

"Cut that crap out. That's not even a poem. I coulda knocked that out in my sleep. You'd think Gwen Brooks was some sort of genius." Then she stomped away, this time into the kitchen. I heard her hands smack the swinging door hard.

Back in the fourth grade, my teacher would have us

lay our heads on our desks after we came in from recess. She would recite poetry to calm us down and get us ready to learn more science or history. Robert Frost, Emily Dickinson, Countee Cullen, and William Blake— all fine poets whom we should know, she'd say. Well, I knew a real, live poet. I didn't know how fine Cecile's poetry was, but I had seen her writing poems in the kitchen and sometimes on the walls or on cereal boxes. Who else in my classroom could claim they knew a poet and that she was their mother? So, on the afternoon that Robert Frost's horse had clip-clopped through the snow, I'd raised my hand and told the class my mother was a poet. "Now, now, Delphine," Mrs. Peterson said, "nice girls don't tell their classmates lies." She'd kept me after school and told me she knew the truth about how my mother had left home and that wanting a mother was no excuse for dreaming one up. I couldn't leave the classroom until I'd written "I will not tell lies in class" twenty-five times on the blackboard. And then I'd had to erase the board clean.

Vonetta sulked something pitiful when Cecile told her to cut it out. Vonetta only heard that her recitation stunk. She wasn't thinking about how Gwendolyn Brooks was a great Negro poet and that Cecile, also called Nzila, was printing her own poems in her kitchen.

Last year, Vonetta practiced her curtsying more than she practiced her wings and time steps for the Tip Top Tap recital. She fell on her fanny in the middle of her solo and was miserable for days. Usually I'd pick up Vonetta's broken spirits until she was once again crowy and showy, but now I let her sulk after she received no praise from Cecile. Serves you right, I thought. Just to be evil, I rubbed it in with an insult.

"I don't know why your lip is hanging," I said. "You're just like her."

We both knew which *her* I meant. I said that to make her feel mad on top of being hurt. Just like I know how to lift my sisters up, I also know how to needle them just right.

"Am not."

"Are too."

We did a few rounds of that, then a final "Not" and "Too."

"Okay, Vonetta. Suppose you were going to be on TV."

She perked up on that one.

"Playing Tinker Bell on *Walt Disney's Wonderful World of Color*. But it was PTA Night. Or School Talent Night. And your little girl—"

"Lootie Belle," Fern added in.

"Lootie Belle," I picked up, glad to have Fern's support, "had a part in *The Itsy Bitsy Spider*."

"In her Itsy Bitsy Spider costume."

"And she'd been practicing her Itsy Bitsy Spider song and dance for days."

"Weeks."

"A whole two months. The Itsy Bitsy Spider—"

"Went up the waterspout." I knew I could count on Fern to climb high with her tiny, sweet voice.

Vonetta sat there defiant, unmoved, proving my point. It was like looking dead at Cecile.

"A shiny white Cadillac comes to carry you off to be Tinker Bell on TV. But your precious little girl—"

"Lootie Belle!"

"Lootie Belle is standing at the door in her costume, waiting for you to take her to School Talent Night. What would you do?"

"That's easy," Vonetta said. "I'd get in the shiny white Cadillac with my matching vanity bag and luggage."

"And what about your little girl in her costume?" I asked.

"Yeah. What about Lootie Bell in her costume, wanting to dance for her mama?"

Each and every one of us knew the feeling of having no mother clapping for us in the audience. Only Big Ma and sometimes Papa when he came home from work in time.

Crowy and showy Vonetta said, "First of all, I wouldn't dare name her anything as silly as Lootie Belle. And my little girl would be happy I was a Disneyland movie star. She would tell her jealous friends at school, 'There goes my mother on TV. I'll bet your mother just fries pork chops and wrings wet clothes. My mother is on TV flying around in blue fairy dust, waving a magical wand in a cute sparkly outfit.'"

The magic of Disneyland had won Fern over to Vonetta's side. It was all of that blue fairy dust and magical-wand stuff. Fern's eyes twinkled as she imagined having a colored fairy mother. I was looking to get Vonetta's goat, but I only ended up losing Fern. And Vonetta was her old self.

"And that's why you're like Cecile. You want to be a fairy on TV more than you care how your kids will feel and if they miss you."

"Do not" and "Do too" went on between us until Cecile stomped back to the room and said, "Cut that crap out!"

Movable Type

We had another long day at the Center. When I came into the kitchen to make spaghetti that evening, there was a stool by the stove. It was like everything else Cecile brought into her green stucco house. Secondhand. Still, it was unexpected, and I welcomed it. I normally stood by the stove quietly while the food cooked. My feet always ached, but I never complained. Instead, I shifted my weight from one foot to the other and learned to make quick-cooking meals. Cecile had allowed me inside her kitchen. She'd let me cook dinner, wash dishes, and clean up after myself. But she didn't really want me in there with her. She didn't want me stretching my neck over her way, ripping open the peace with any talking.

The stool made things different. It was an invitation for me to sit down and be there. Not talk. Just cook. Be. As the spaghetti boiled, pictures flashed in and out of my mind. Flashes of sitting with Cecile and being quiet. It was the welcome that had brought me back. That I'd sat with her before and it was all right. Not in this kitchen, but in the kitchen in Brooklyn. Back when Sarah Vaughan filled the house with her smoky voice, Vonetta was far away crying to be picked up, and Cecile's stomach was big with Fern.

I wouldn't be exaggerating if I said I was born knowing what to do when I sat with Cecile: Don't cry. Stay quiet. Want nothing. I could talk, but I'd learned that, as long as I was quiet, I was allowed to stay with her while she tapped against the wall with her pencil, wrote and wrote and said her rhymes over and over. Don't cry. Stay quiet. Want nothing.

Then Fern had come, and days later Cecile left. Big Ma had moved in and told Pa, "That gal's dumb as a dry pump," meaning me. Cecile wouldn't have minded if I had been born deaf and mute, but Cecile was gone. Big Ma was another story. I quickly learned to speak up around Big Ma.

After we ate our spaghetti, I washed the dishes and wiped the sink down.

Cecile said, "I'd let you help me if your hands were clean."

My hands were already clean. I had just finished washing dishes. But I soaped them with dish-washing liquid, then rinsed and dried them.

"Stand over here."

I stood where she told me. For a long while that was all she said, that I stand right there. I looked down on a flat frame with wooden blocks. On the wooden blocks were metal letters facing backward. Backward? They spelled out words, line by line. But you would have to be able to read backward to read the lines.

I wanted to be able to read them. On the counter next to the printing machine was a newly inked sheet of paper with the words printed in the right direction.

Movable Type

Push here
I move
there
Push
there
I move
two squares over
Buy those squares
from under my
feet
I land on

the free square.
Raise my
Rent
I
Pica
Elite
Courier
Sans Serif
Pack light. Leave swift.
I'm that type.
I move.

NZILA

She took the sheet and hung it up to dry.

"I'm going to press down and roll the crank," she said. I figured I would catch on.

She turned the lever on the side of the printing machine. Her weight pressed into the machine and down on the metal and paper. The rollers spun slowly. The paper pushed its way out onto the tray of backward letters.

When the paper was fully inked, I believed she was pleased. Not that she was smiling or jolly or singing. But she liked what she had done. She studied her printed sheet and held it up to the light. The poem in black ink. Her name, Nzila, in special-shaped letters: large, curved, lovely, and green.

I thought about Cecile's poem. I figured it was about how she was the type to not be still. But I believed she liked this green stucco house. I think she liked being in this kitchen, mothering and praying over this big machine and these blocks of backward letters. This was Cecile being happy.

"See this here?"

I must have made a move like I was going to touch it.

Cecile spoke sharply. "I said 'see,' not 'touch.' See."

I nodded and put my hands behind my back. I was used to busy hands. To doing. I did what she said. I looked.

"Those are the rollers. You feed the paper through the rollers. You feed it even. If it's crooked, it's a waste of paper. You crank it steady or it's a waste of paper. Waste of ink."

I watched her feed the paper between the rollers and turn the crank. Each time the ink spread evenly on the paper. She hung each sheet to dry.

"Go 'head." She pointed to the paper and the rollers and the crank.

I almost didn't move.

"Come on. Let's see if you can follow directions."

I took a sheet from the paper stack and held it from end to end so it would go in even. No matter how much I told myself to keep steady, my hands made the paper shake. I was mad at my own hands. I didn't want Cecile to think I was afraid of doing wrong, but I was.

I didn't look up at her to see if I had done right in her eyes. I just did what she said and turned the crank slow, hard, and steady until the paper came out on the other side, I hoped, fully inked.

She held up my newly printed sheet and pointed to a spot on the *N* in "Nzila" that missed the rollers. She shook her head. "A waste of paper."

San Francisco Treat

Cecile didn't care where we went or what we did on Saturdays and Sundays, as long as we stayed far away from her peace and quiet. Our first weekend, we had played Go Fish and tic-tac-toe in our room and waited for Cecile to announce that we were going to some adventurous place that existed only in California. By the second weekend I knew we had to have a plan. Since the sun rose high that Saturday, I figured it was a good day to go to the beach and collect seashells for souvenirs. Vonetta, Fern, and I had put on our bathing suits and sunglasses, and I'd asked Cecile to take us to the beach. I had never spoken Martian to someone and had them give me the look that could only be given to a

Martian. Instead of answering our question, Cecile gave us a look that said, *Who are you and what planet did y'all come from?* I ended up taking my sisters to the city pool, where we swam and splashed around without thinking about all that chlorine water knotting up our hair. When we'd come back to her house smelling like chlorine, I'd asked Cecile if I could use her hot comb to press our hair, seeing how knotty it got.

I'd expected she'd say no outright because I'd smoke up her precious workplace with hair burning from the hot comb. In fact, I'd expected a no followed by an "I didn't send for y'all in the first place." It hadn't occurred to me that Cecile didn't own a hot comb or curling iron, even though that fact was as big and thick as her unpressed braids. She'd said, "Naughty? Your hair ain't naughty. It ain't misbehaving. It's doing what God meant it to do." That would have been news to Big Ma. We never entered the house of God without our hair pressed and smelling of Dixie Peach hair grease.

For our third Saturday in Oakland I had a better plan. I told my sisters, "We're going on an excursion." Miss Merriam Webster would have been proud. Excursion. To Vonetta's and Fern's uncomprehending faces, I said, "We're taking a bus ride to our own adventure." It didn't make sense to fly three thousand miles to the land of Mickey Mouse, movie stars, and all-year sun and not see anything but Black Panthers, police cars, and poor black people. I wasn't foolish enough to set out for Hollywood, Disneyland, or the beach where they filmed *Happening '68* with rock and rollers like Paul Revere and the Raiders. Instead, I planned that we would spend our nearly last Saturday in California traveling across the bay to San Francisco to ride a cable car and see Chinatown, Fisherman's Wharf, and the Golden Gate Bridge. Now, that was an excursion worthy of a back-to-school essay. Even if we didn't have a camera to take pictures of us on our adventure, we would know we'd been there.

I told my sisters, "Don't say a word. Just let me do all the talking." Even though I knew Cecile didn't care, I didn't want her to suddenly take an interest in us and ask a lot of questions. If she asked questions, I'd have to spin a lot of straw; and I couldn't spin a lot of straw and look her in the face the way I'd like to. Like I'm eleven going on twelve and I know what I'm doing.

"Cecile, we need money. I have all-day activities planned, and we have to eat while we're out doing our activities."

"Yeah, gotta eat."

I turned to Fern. *Don't say no more, Fern.* She got it.

"If I pour cereal for them before we go," I said, "I'll only need change for the bus, and some lunch money, and a little extra if you want us gone long."

Cecile almost raised an eyebrow but not quite. She figured we were up to something but probably didn't want to know the details.

154

She reached into her man's pants and poured a lot of nickels, dimes, pennies, and some quarters into my hands. I needed both hands to get every coin. She dealt out eleven single dollars from a wad of bills and gave me those also. I was so giddy about having all of that money, I just dumped it in my shoulder bag. I could sort it out later. Just by the weight of the silver and copper I knew we had more than the fifteen dollars I'd counted on us getting.

I ate my cereal and washed the dishes with my shoulder bag slung around my neck Brooklyn-style. The best way to lose your money is to hold your bag off the shoulder, but this way, with the bag slung crosswise, you were ready for anything.

As we were walking out the door excited about our excursion, Cecile called out, "I'm not coming down to no police station if you're out there stealing. Y'all have to spend the night in jail." That was as good a "Be safe and have a good time" as we were going to get from Cecile. We took it and left.

Outside, the yards and streets were filled with screaming kids playing. It was all I could do to keep Vonetta and Fern in line for my fully planned excursion. I had worked too hard writing everything down to have them not want to go. I had asked Sister Pat about the bus and cable car. I had gotten all the sightseeing information from the library. I wasn't about to let a kickball game and some Barbie tea parties throw mile-long pouts on Vonetta and Fern because they wanted to stay here in black, poor Oakland.

Then the worst possible thing happened. Hirohito came rambling up to us on his homemade go-kart. He skidded to a stop using his high-top sneakers, right at Vonetta's feet. She squealed and laughed and said, "Whatcha know, Hirohito?" That was some cute thing she and Janice Ankton came up with. I was sick of hearing it.

"Delphine. Want to watch me fly down that hill?"

"No," I said, while my sisters screamed, *"Yes!"*

I glanced at my Timex. *Don't stand there watching Hirohito on his go-kart,* it said. *The East Bay bus leaves in twelve minutes. You don't have time for that.*

Vonetta and Fern folded their arms and wouldn't budge. They watched Hirohito do that run and flop onto the flying T and go bumpity-bump down the hill. When he neared the end of the hill, he dragged his sneakers like Fred Flintstone and came to a full stop. Then he jumped up and turned to us, waving. Vonetta and Fern waved back.

"Let's see him do it again," Vonetta said.

"It's a boy going down the hill," I said. "We seen it already. Let's go."

I couldn't say it was thrilling, how he jumped on that board thing and rolled down the hill, twisting the T left and right and then swerving it around. I couldn't say how I admired him for not crying about his father being in prison and for trying to be a normal kid. If you wanted to call Hirohito Woods normal. I certainly didn't want Vonetta to get the wrong idea and think I was as stuck on Hirohito as she and Janice were. Because I wasn't. He was just a boy, and I didn't want to miss the bus to our adventure.

Our bus pushed out of poor and black Oakland, where lines formed for free breakfasts and men stood around because there were no jobs and too much liquor. We were glad to be going. Each of us looked out and off into different directions, taking in all that we could. Finally we were on our way to an adventure.

I watched Fern, glued to the bus window and singing to herself. I wondered if she missed Miss Patty Cake at all. How she loved, loved, loved Miss Patty Cake long before she could walk. She teethed on Miss Patty Cake's arms and legs, ate her hair when she didn't know better, squeezed her, slept with her, fed her, and sang to her. Seven years of loving Miss Patty Cake and now not one mention of her.

I can study every move Fern makes and still not completely know her. There are just things I don't understand about her the way I understand Vonetta. After Miss Patty Cake had been damaged and put away, I slept lightly, expecting Fern to awaken during the night missing her truelove. Not that I wanted Fern to be heartbroken. I didn't want her to love someone all her life and then not love or want them at all. Even if her someone was a doll.

That was no way to be.

I wanted to say something to Fern, but then she cupped her hand around her mouth and squealed an Ooh! like she'd seen something bad, like a naked lady running down the street. It was that kind of an "ooh" squeal.

"What, Fern?"

Her eyes stayed big, her hand over her mouth. Vonetta and I kept going, "What, Fern? What, Fern?"

She swallowed a gulp of air and uncupped her mouth. "I saw something." She said it again, and had gone from agog to being pleased with herself. "I saw something." She clapped to the beat. *Clap, clap, clap, clap.*

No matter how much we asked, Fern shook her head no, clapped her hands, and sang her song: "I saw something."

Fern was pleased she had seen something, Vonetta was sure she hadn't seen a thing, and I remembered he had said "Delphine." *Delphine. Want to watch me fly down that hill?*

Wish We
Had a Camera

Once we arrived in San Francisco, Fern stopped singing "I saw something," and we stopped asking her to tell us what she had seen. We got off the bus and were greeted by hippies hanging out by the bus stop. It wasn't right to stare at them like they were in an exhibit, but we couldn't help it. We didn't see many hippies in Brooklyn, not where we lived; and there was a whole tribe of them before us. All kinds of mostly white hippies with long, hanging hair. You couldn't miss the guy in the green, red, and white Mexican poncho or the moppy hair covering his face. I'd have called it an Afro except it was on a white guy's head. I wondered if that made a difference.

The hippies sat on the grass. One read a small book.

Three girls swayed while Poncho Man played his guitar. They must have been out protesting and were done for the day. Their signs lay on the grass: PEACE. BAN THE DRAFT. MAKE LOVE, NOT WAR.

I wished we had a camera.

"Peace, sweet soul sisters." Poncho Man dipped his head as if pointing to his open guitar case.

I don't know what made me say it, but instead of "Groovy, man" or "Peace," I said, "Power to the people."

Then Vonetta said, "Free Huey."

And Fern said, "Yeah. Free Huey Newton."

That was when we met her. The Flower Girl. We had finally seen one! There were all kinds of songs on the radio about hippie girls with flowers in their hair. She had daisies in her hair; and she drifted over to us, her eyes all dreamy as she danced in her flowing, paint-splattered dress. She took a daisy from her hair and gave it to Fern. Then she had to give one to Vonetta, because Vonetta wasn't about to be overlooked.

"Peace is power, sweet soul sisters."

We wanted to crack up but saved that for later. We took the flowers and dropped two nickels and five pennies in Poncho Man's guitar case. Even though I could have figured it out, I asked him where Grant Street was. He pointed east. We gave the hippies the peace sign and the power sign and walked over to Grant Street.

We were excited by the sight of metal rails in the street.

The cable car was second on my list of activities. Our first activity was sightseeing in Chinatown.

You know when you're in Chinatown. The buildings are just like they are in China. "That's a temple," I told my sisters. I had seen the pictures in *National Geographic* magazine and in the encyclopedia. Nothing compared to actually seeing the roofs, like tiled lamp shades or hats. Dragons of every color. Gold. Red. Blue. Green. Pink. Big heads with large fangs, big eyes, monstrous paws. We needed a camera.

We shared a plate of dumplings and drank free tea. None of us could keep the dumplings between the chopsticks, so we used forks. After that we found a place where all they did was make fortune cookies. They let us come in and watch the ladies slip fortunes inside flat yellow cookie dough, then fold the dough over. We bought ten fortune cookies for a dollar. Our first fortune said, *You will travel far*. I said, "We already did." Still, I put each pink-and-white strip of paper in my shoulder bag as souvenirs. Now we could say we had real Chinese fortune cookies in Chinatown.

We gawked at all the window offerings. Green statues that I learned were carved jade. China dolls. Fans. Silk and satin dresses with Nehru collars. I almost felt bad about not having more money to spend.

"I want a kimono," Vonetta declared.

"Me too. A blue one," Fern said.

"A kimono is Japanese," I said, as if I knew the difference. "And we're in Chinatown."

"It's the same thing," Vonetta said. "And I want one."

"It is not," I told her. "And we have five dollars exactly for souvenirs, so you're out of luck."

While we were arguing about what was Chinese and what was Japanese, I noticed this family of five tall blond people standing near us. I didn't eyeball them dead-on, but I knew they were staring at us.

My heart thumped fast. It was happening. That bad thing that happened to kids who went on excursions without their mother. I tried to shush Vonetta, who thought she was winning our disagreement. I had to get my sisters away from these starers. And then, what would I tell the police when they asked about our mother? We were cooked.

When I turned, I found the five people smiling at us, their faces made long by high cheekbones and long, white teeth. They waved.

I'd seen white people before. On TV. At school. Everywhere. These people didn't look like any white people I had ever seen. Even their skin was paler, their hair more white than yellow. I listened as they spoke to one another, probably about us, using flugal, schlugal words. Then, instead of taking pictures of all the Chinese people and the temples and dragons, they pointed their cameras at us. Vonetta started to pose movie star–style with one hand behind her head and the other on her slim hip. I grabbed Vonetta's and Fern's hands and said, "Come on."

I checked my Timex. It was almost one o'clock. That meant our time in Chinatown was up and we had to go on to our next activity. A ride on the cable car. We dashed over to where metal rails ran along the street and waited. Sure enough, at one o'clock on the nose we were on to our next activity. A cable car ride from the tip-top of Chinatown all the way down to Fisherman's Wharf. We climbed aboard, and I paid our fare. We stood because standing would be more fun going down that hill. And what a hill it was. It was a thrilling look down, down, down. The streets rolled like a dancing dragon. Hirohito didn't know the first thing about a hill.

We needed a camera to get this hill. How steep. How long. We rode it all the way down to the wharf, cheering with every clang of the bell.

We were now near the wharf. There were palm trees—real palm trees with sturdy trunks. Down here, palm trees made sense. They stood as palm trees were supposed to stand. Reaching up to the sun, branches spread out wide. Not like a sickly child, too small and slouched over in someone's yard in black Oakland.

When we got off, we could see the Golden Gate Bridge perfectly well, but we took turns looking through the telescope right there on the walkway. Gazing out to the bridge, I felt what I almost felt on the airplane. It was the pure excitement of seeing the world. Even the seagulls were seagullier than the ones that flew and squawked around Coney Island. These wide-winged birds seemed bigger and majestic, both close-up and far away. Or maybe it was that we could see and smell the ocean and the tar, salt, and wood from the wharf. I breathed in deep to get it all. Too bad there was no way to capture the wharf smell in a jar to take with me. For a minute I forgot I was with my sisters. Then I remembered what Papa had said, and I stopped myself from falling into the whiff of salt air and flying off with the seagulls like some dreamy flower girl. I was happy to be there, and that had to be good enough. There was no need to get glaze eyed and forgetful.

We stopped in a gift shop on the wharf. The man behind the counter set his eyes on us really hard. At first I thought it was because we were by ourselves, so I whispered to Vonetta and Fern to be extra well behaved. But then I heard Cecile's last words in my head. His hard stare was for the other reason store clerks' eyes never let up. We were black kids, and he expected us to be in his gift shop to steal. When he asked us what we wanted, I answered him like I was at the Center, repeating after Sister Mukumbu or Sister Pat: "We are citizens, and we demand respect."

I grabbed Fern by the hand and said, "Let's go."

I had that Black Panther stuff in me, and it was pouring out at every turn. I figured it was all right. Papa wouldn't have wanted me to spend our money where we weren't treated with respect. But I was sure Big Ma would have wanted us to say "Yes, sir" and "Please, sir" to show him we were just as civilized as everyone else.

We walked farther down the wharf and found an old lady with a wooden cart to buy our souvenirs from. She carried mostly postcards, silver spoons, thimbles, and tiny drinking glasses that said WELCOME TO SAN FRANCISCO. Her cart wasn't as nice as the gift shop, but she was toothless and happy to get our nickels and dimes. Since we didn't have a camera, I thought buying ten postcards for fifty cents would be the next best thing. I told my sisters to each pick out three postcards. One to keep as a reminder of our San Francisco excursion, one to mail to Pa and Big Ma, and one to send to Uncle Darnell in Vietnam. I'd figure out later what we'd do with the leftover postcard. At least now we finally had something to show for flying all the way to California.

We took the cable car to the bus stop and took the East Bay bus back to Oakland. We talked and talked about all the things we had seen and the hippies and the tall blond white people and the red and golden dragons and the steep hills and the cable car and seagulls and dumplings and everything! Wouldn't Cecile be surprised when we told her where we went?

Then I felt bad because we didn't get her anything from the souvenir cart. I hadn't thought of her at all, and guilt began to have its way with me. I told my sisters, "We're selfish. We didn't buy anything for Cecile." Before we got too quiet, stewing in our selfishness, Vonetta said, "She wouldn't want it anyway." Good old Vonetta! Fern and I agreed with her. "Surely wouldn't."

In a way, I was glad to be back in black Oakland, the sun still shining. As much as I loved our adventure, I was always on the lookout in between just looking. Here, I knew where everything was: the Center, the park, the library, the city pool, Safeway, and Mean Lady Ming's. No one stared, unless they were staring because they didn't like your shoes or your hairstyle. Not because you were black or they thought you were stealing. As much as we needed to go off and have our California adventure, it was nice to be back. Even if it wasn't our real home. I still carried my shoulder bag Brooklyn-style, but it was now lighter and I wasn't worried.

We stopped inside Mean Lady Ming's and gave her all the change we had left except for two dollar bills. "What can we get with this?"

Mean Lady Ming yelled something mean back to the kitchen, and in ten minutes we had a brown bag smelling of fried rice and chicken wings. I figured one day of take-out food wouldn't hurt anything, but honestly, I was too tired and happy to cook. I was anxious to tell Cecile all about our vacation day. I wanted to show off how well I had planned everything down to the minute, that I knew what to do; and I wanted to see if she cared.

We were a block away from the green stucco house, chatting and laughing. Then we stopped walking. All three of us. There were three police cars parked outside of Cecile's house. One in the driveway and two along the curb. Policemen lined the walk. Lights flashed on top of their cars onto the streets. Red, white, and blue lights everywhere. We inched up, the happiness knocked out of us.

Cecile and two Black Panthers. Hands behind their backs. Handcuffed. Being led out of the house and down the walkway. I could hardly breathe.

The Clark Sisters

We were only a few houses away when Vonetta said, "Hey!"
I could feel Fern wanting to leap out, ready to call out, but
I pulled her back and shushed them both.

"What about their rights?" Vonetta said.

"Yeah. We know about rights," Fern said.

"Just *shhhh*," I said. My heart was pounding. "They're
Panthers. They're grown," I said, although I didn't think
Cecile was truly a Panther. "They know their rights."

"But—"

I told Vonetta to be quiet. We were now coming up on
the house and all the patrol-car lights flashing.

Cecile was almost as tall as the policeman who walked
her to a flashing patrol car. He bent slightly to tell her

something. She said loudly, "Kids? I don't have no kids. They belong to the Clarks down the street." She wouldn't even look at us.

We were now closer, where the police could really see us. With my shoulders, arms, and legs exactly like hers, Vonetta's I-don't-care eyes exactly like hers, and Fern a smaller version of Vonetta and me, I said, "She's not our mother. I'm Delphine Clark."

"I'm Vonetta Clark."

"I'm Fern Clark."

"And we live down the street."

"With Pa and Big Ma."

"Yeah. Down the street in a blue stucco house."

"Not with this lady," I said.

"Not with her."

"Surely don't."

They had already pushed Cecile down into the back-seat of the car.

I said to my sisters without looking at Cecile, "Come on." We walked past our mother. Walked with our bag of fried rice and chicken wings as far as we could without looking back, my heart still pounding and the smell of the fried food making me sick.

Why had the police arrested Cecile? She wrote "Send us back to Africa" poems and "Movable Type" poems. She didn't write "Off the Pig" poems and "Kill Whitey" poems, that is, if writing poems were a crime.

It was just as Sister Mukumbu and Crazy Kelvin were trying to teach us. In Oakland they arrested you for being something. Saying something. If you were a freedom fighter, sooner or later you would be arrested.

Fern asked, "Why'd she say she didn't have no kids?"

"She had to," I said.

"Why?"

"They would have taken us away, split us up, and put us in juvie or something."

Fern said, "I don't want to go to juvie."

Vonetta said, "She sure said it really easy. 'Kids? I don't have no kids.' It was like she said, 'Cooties? I don't have no cooties.'"

I reminded her, "And we said we were the Clarks real quick. Real easy."

"I was following you," Vonetta said.

"Me too," Fern said.

"Well, we had to say that. Did you want them to send us to juvenile hall? Or call Pa and Big Ma and worry them to death? We'd have to wait in juvie hall until Pa or Big Ma came from New York to get us. You wouldn't like juvie hall. It's just like jail."

By the time we turned around and started back, the police cars had driven off with Cecile and the two Black Panthers.

I let us in. I couldn't tell from the living room what had happened between Cecile, the police, and the two Black Panthers. The door had not been kicked in like it had been at Hirohito's house. Cecile didn't have much in her house to begin with. Then I pushed open the door to the kitchen. Out of habit Vonetta and Fern stayed in the living room until they heard me gasp. They followed quickly behind me and timidly peered in.

Black and red ink was smeared across the floor. Torn and scuffed-up white paper wings covered the floor. Drawers had been ripped out of cabinets. Large and tiny blocks of metal letters had flown everywhere. Blocks of metal *E*s, *S*s, *A*s, and *T*s. Paper, ink everywhere. The printing machine toppled over. Rollers knocked out. Legs from my second-hand stool cracked and split off from the wooden seat.

All we could do was take it in. Vonetta and Fern were seeing the inside of the kitchen—Cecile's workplace—for the first time. I was imagining what had happened. How Cecile didn't want them in her house. In her workplace. Where she only allowed me, and only at a distance. That the police might have touched her papers or picked up her letters with clumsy cop hands. Cecile might have gone crazy like I knew she could have, instead of saying "I'm a citizen, and I have rights." She and the Black Panthers might have demanded to see the policemen's search warrant. She might have reached out to protect her poems.

The broken stool told me more than I wanted to know.

I found three forks. Two on the floor and one in the sink. I washed them along with three plates, and we went back out to the living room. Vonetta spread Cecile's tablecloth, and we sat down to eat. I said the blessing, asking God to protect Cecile while she was under arrest, and then we ate. Mean Lady Ming had thrown in two extra chicken wings, and that was good because we were hungry. Hungry, shook up, and tired.

"We have to clean up Cecile's kitchen before she comes home."

"Why?" Vonetta asked. "We didn't mess it up."

"We surely didn't," Fern said.

"We're cleaning the kitchen just because."

"Because?" they said together.

"Because it should look right when Cecile comes home tomorrow."

I expected a lot of lip from Vonetta, with Fern on her side. I expected us to go back and forth, them saying "Oh no, we're not," while I said "Oh yes, we are."

Instead Vonetta asked, "What if she doesn't come home tomorrow? What if they keep her locked up like Brother Woods?"

"Yeah," Fern said. "They could keep her and never let her go."

They were right. The police could keep Cecile for days. Even longer.

My sisters waited for my answer, but for the first time I had no straw to spin. I could only clear away the food, plates, and forks.

I Birthed a Nation

I didn't care what Big Ma said about scrubbing like a gal from a one-cow town near Prattville, Alabama. Only turpentine could wipe away the black and red ink that had seeped into the linoleum floor tiles. I wiped up all the ink I could before we went to bed that night. Everything else—the paper, the metal letters, and the mess the police made—would have to wait until we woke up. The day had been just too long.

When I pushed the kitchen door open in the morning, the room didn't look any better. Streams of sunlight shot through Cecile's cheap curtains and pointed out *Delphine, you got a whole lot of work to do. A lot, girl.*

I was set to do it. Pick up, put away, clean and mop

everything. But I was still tired, which didn't make sense to me. I had slept even longer than usual. Yet all I could do was sigh heavily when I saw the inside of Cecile's kitchen. Everything that made me tall, able, and ready to do what had to be done made me sigh. I picked up the broken stool—the seat, legs, and scattered wood chips—then brought the pieces out to the trash can. There was nothing I could do about the printing machine. It was too heavy. I used all my strength to sit it upright on the floor. I wiped the rollers and laid them on top of the machine. Then I called Vonetta and Fern out of bed and put them to work helping me.

Without a squawk Vonetta gathered up all of the paper—and there was a heavy snowfall of paper. She made different piles. The scuffed and dirty papers went in one pile. The rally flyers went in another. The sheets of poetry with Cecile's poet name, Nzila, printed on the bottom went in another. Vonetta spent most of her time separating out the different poems; and in between, she read them.

I had Fern hunt around the floor for the metal letters and put them up on the table where the printing machine once sat. I never realized how many metal letters Cecile had in the drawers and kitchen cabinets. She had boxes and boxes of them. Large and small capitals and lowercase letters. Different sizes and types of *T*s. Some more boxy, some more curved. Some slanted but not like Hirohito's eyes. Slanted like a leaning flower stem on a sunny day. Some *O*s and

*Q*s and *C*s long and narrow. Others round and squat. All sizes, all types. All over. Was this "movable type," like her poem? Each letter free to be flung to all four corners?

Then Fern found two of Cecile's special letters. The ones she used for her poetry name. The *N* and the *Z*. I found the *I*, *L*, and *A*. I polished those with the dish towel. These were a special type. Tall and curved, hooks on the ends, the *Z* coiled back to strike like a snake. In all her collection, these were the only letters of this kind. I wouldn't be surprised if she had thrown out the other twenty-one letters, or if these were the only ones she had bought. Just so that only her name could be spelled out with these letters.

I mopped the floor once the papers, letter blocks, and mess had been cleared away. We brought all of the letters and boxes into the living room and spread out the table-cloth. We spent the rest of the afternoon sorting through Cecile's letters. It was like a game. Finding the right letters, the right type, the right size. I put the "Nzila" letters in one box by themselves. We didn't know if that was the right way, but at least it was a way. Vonetta took out one of Cecile's poems and read it to us.

"I think it's about us," Vonetta said. "Look at the title: 'I Birthed a Nation.'"

"You might be right," I said.

"Surely might be."

Vonetta said, "We should do this poem." She read it again. It was a good poem for reciting out loud. The same way "We Real Cool" was a good poem for reciting. And then we joined her. Each of us taking a line, one after the other. Then we chose our own stanza but recited the last one together. We decided Cecile's poem was in a way like "Dry Your Eyes." We decided that it was about Mother Africa losing her children like Cecile had lost us. I didn't remind my sisters that Cecile had left us.

Then there was a knock on the door and we froze. We remembered we were in Cecile's green stucco house where the Black Panthers had come and the police had come and Cecile had been arrested and we were supposed to be the Clark sisters down the street. Not Cecile's daughters reciting her poems in her house.

We became like spies. I mouthed, "Be quiet," and hoped whoever was at the door would go away. They knocked again. I put my finger to my lips. Then Vonetta popped up her head and looked through the curtain.

"It's Hirohito!" she cried out. "With an Oriental lady."

I didn't know what to be. Mad at Vonetta for being her Hirohito-crazy self. Relieved it was Hirohito. Nervous about the lady.

I cracked the door open.

Hirohito said loudly, "Open up, Delphine. It's me. And my mom."

His mother? I looked at my sisters. My sisters looked at

me. Vonetta flapped her arms wildly, wanting me to open the door. I didn't want to, but I did anyway. Hirohito's mother was holding a pan with tinfoil over it. Then I felt rude and stupid. "Hello," I said. "You can come in, but my mother isn't home."

I had never said that to anyone before. "My mother," in a real way.

Vonetta and Fern were all smiles.

I closed the door quickly after they stepped inside.

"I know your mother isn't home, Delphine," Hirohito's mother said. "I know."

"She'll be home soon," I said. "Maybe tomorrow." The truth was, I didn't know anything about Cecile and why they had taken her or how long she would be gone.

"Look. My mom made this food, and I'm hungry. Let's eat."

To that, Mrs. Woods gave Hirohito a slap against the head and said something to him in Japanese. He said, "Mom, I'm hungry."

I was embarrassed that we didn't have tables or chairs. I certainly didn't want that going around the Center tomorrow. We had been laughed at enough for one summer. But Hirohito's mother didn't blink once when I said, "We always eat on the floor." She put the tins on the floor while I got the plates, forks, and the biggest serving spoon I could find. Vonetta and Fern just giggled and kept asking Hirohito to say something in Japanese. He rolled his eyes.

We sat down and ate fried pork chops, rice, and string beans. I wanted to eat nicely like Mrs. Woods ate, but I ate hungrily like Cecile. Hirohito ate hungrily also. He scooped more rice and string beans onto his plate, and seeing that I was nearly done, he scooped more rice and string beans onto mine. I couldn't look up at him. I just ate.

Mrs. Woods said, "We know the same things. We have to stick together."

Stores of
the No Sayers

I gave what few flyers Cecile had printed up to Sister Mukumbu. She, Sister Pat, Crazy Kelvin, the ladies who served breakfast, and everyone else all knew that Nzila had been arrested. Sister Mukumbu said we should stay with her until Nzila was released.

It was funny how things changed. If Cecile had been arrested when we first arrived in Oakland, I would have called Pa, and Pa would have made sure my sisters and I were on a plane back to New York. Nothing would have made me happier than to leave Cecile and Oakland back then. But we hadn't gotten what we came for. We didn't really know our mother, and I couldn't leave without knowing who she was. I certainly didn't want to tell Big

Ma that everything she had said about Cecile for the past seven years was right. That Cecile was no kind of mother and had gotten herself locked up to prove it. It was bad enough to hear Big Ma supposing out loud every kind of selfish trouble Cecile was tangled up in. Day in, day out, I'd never hear the end of it. And there was no telling Big Ma that Cecile was a freedom fighter, oppressed by the Man. Day in, day out, Big Ma would give my ear a hurting over Cecile.

No. I couldn't call Pa yet. What if Cecile were released tomorrow?

I thanked Sister Mukumbu for her offer and told her as quietly as I could that we were staying with Hirohito and his mother. I certainly didn't want Eunice and her sisters to know we were staying at the Woods' house. Although Vonetta promised to keep her mouth shut, I didn't think she could hold it in. Anything to make Janice jealous. "Our mother will expect us to be home when they let her out. She won't be too happy hunting around town looking for us if we're not home."

Sister Mukumbu said we would be safer with Mrs. Woods than by ourselves. Sister Pat added, "The Man is still watching the house."

I asked Sister Mukumbu why our mother had been arrested in the first place. She said the police were really after the two who had been arrested with her. She also said our mother helped to spread the word by volunteering her printing services. "Information is power," she told me as if we were having a lesson. "Keeping the people informed keeps the people empowered."

Cecile wasn't exactly like Hirohito's father, going around spreading the word and telling the truth. She fussed about printing anything other than her poetry. I didn't tell Sister Mukumbu that. And honestly, I believed she said that about Nzila giving power to the people to make me feel good about seeing my mother being taken away in handcuffs.

Crazy Kelvin held up his fist and said, "Stay strong, my black sisters. Hold your heads up."

Vonetta gave him the power sign back, but Fern pointed at him and said, "What's wrong with this picture?"

He laughed like Fern was a silly little girl. To someone Kelvin's age, she was just that. A silly little girl. To his chuckle, Fern said, "Good boy, Fido." Then she barked. *"Arf! Arf!"*

Vonetta and I were embarrassed and puzzled by Fern calling Kelvin out like he was a dog and then barking at him. I pulled her away.

Fern laughed and hummed her bus song—"I saw something"—and clapped her hands.

After we practiced being led to freedom by Janice Ankton as Harriet Tubman, Sister Mukumbu announced we would do community work. We would take Sister Nzila's flyers out into the community and ask store owners to display them in their windows. Each of us had to present ourselves to the manager or owner. We were to be respectful and clear: "Good afternoon. We are from the People's Center summer camp and are participating in the people's rally. We are asking you to help the people of your community by displaying our flyer for the people's rally this Saturday." Older kids, like Eunice, Hirohito, and me, also included information about free sickle cell anemia testing, voter registration, free shoes for the poor, supporting Huey Newton, and changing the park's name to the Bobby Hutton Park. If store managers said yes, we were to thank them and tape a flyer to their window. If they said no, we were to leave just as respectfully as we came. "Heads up high. Walking tall," Sister Mukumbu said.

Hirohito was up first. He went to Saint Augustine's Church and gave his presentation to a priest he seemed to know. Hirohito had it easy. The priest seemed to be only too happy to take Hirohito's flyer. It figured. The church served free breakfasts and gave away bags of food to poor people. They were, as Sister Pat might say, "down with the cause," or as Huey might say, "carrying the weight." Still, Hirohito congratulated himself as he rejoined the group.

I was supposed to ask Mean Lady Ming, but I knew she would say yes to me. I said, "Fern, Mean Lady Ming likes you. Go get her." I followed behind her but kept my distance. Fern couldn't remember all of her speech, but what she said was good enough. "Good afternoon, Mean Lady Ming. We would like to put the people's flyer in your window for the people's rally this Saturday. Free Huey. Power to the people." Mean Lady Ming wasn't rankled by the name Fern called her. Her complaints, all in Chinese, sounded just like her complaints about customers who wanted extra duck sauce or a free egg roll. That didn't stop her from taking Fern's flyer and taping it up in the window.

Vonetta and Janice Ankton approached the Shabazz Bakery together. Another easy presentation. The bakery had pictures of Malcolm X and Black Power slogans on the wall. It didn't matter to either Vonetta or Janice. They both came out of the bakery waving their arms like home-run hitters.

Black, white, Mexican, or Chinese. Big stores, little stores. Some shook their heads north and south, some shook their heads east and west. There were others who, in the middle of our presentations, simply pointed us to the door. In those cases especially, Sister Mukumbu praised us for how well we presented ourselves and for how we left. Respectfully, with our heads held high.

Both Eunice and I went for the harder ones. Stores of the no sayers. Places where we weren't guaranteed a listen or a smile. We'd both heard no before. The hardened looks of grown-ups who didn't like kids or black people, or kids who were black, were nothing new to us.

After Eunice's third no, Sister Mukumbu pulled her aside for a little chat. Eunice had a hip-switching way about her walk that would have gotten me spoken to but good by Big Ma. When the store managers said no, Eunice would say "Thank you anyway" the same way we'd say "Forget you, forgot you" on the playground. Then she'd walk her hip-switching walk on out of their store.

I said I would go into the Safeway store and find the manager. Surely the grocery store workers had seen my sisters and me skipping through the aisles with our basket. I went up to the manager and said in my cheeriest voice, "Good afternoon. I am from the People's Center summer camp, and I buy dinner groceries at this store." I threw that one in there for good measure. Just as I was telling him about the rally and how good it would be for the community, he said no and something about it being "against store policy." But he did look friendly. He did smile and thank us for shopping at Safeway.

I had no hips to swish away with. Instead, my long legs carried me down the produce aisle, past the bread aisle, and out of Safeway. I had been keeping a list of the east-west no sayers and put Safeway at the very top of it. My sisters, Cecile, and I would eat egg rolls, white rice, bean pies, and fried fish before we spent another penny in the stores of the no sayers.

Glorious Hill

I didn't know which was weirder. Having Hirohito see me in my pajamas or not having any chores to do. I tried to wash dishes and always offered to mop the floor, but for the fifth day in a row, Mrs. Woods said, "Go outside. Play."

I felt like a watcher while Hirohito chased Vonetta and Fern around. I sat on the porch with my book in my lap, glad I'd brought it along. In between turning pages, I'd peek at Vonetta, Fern, and Hirohito playing Mother May I or freeze tag. He knew just how to escape their tags and keep the game going. I could see why Hirohito put up with Vonetta and Janice at the Center. Why he let Fern chase him and tag him "it" when she wasn't fast enough to catch him. Hirohito had no brothers or sisters. He liked being a brother to my sisters and me.

Grateful that Hirohito would soon tire his "sisters" out, I settled into my book on the porch. I could finish the chapter before it was time to come inside. I read my book, bright eyed, breathing heavily, and rooted for Rontu to win against the pack of wild dogs, his former brothers. *Get 'em, Rontu. Get 'em.* I didn't hear the quiet. That the sounds of playing in the yard had stopped. I looked up, and they were all standing around me with Hirohito's go-kart.

"Hey. Delphine."

Vonetta and Fern giggled. Obviously they were a part of Hirohito's plan to sneak up on me. He smiled, pleased to have caught me unaware.

"Want to try out my go-kart?"

I rolled my eyes and tried to appear older. Above playing kid games. "Me? On that thing?"

Vonetta and Fern started screaming that they wanted a ride.

He tapped my sneaker with one of his doggedy hightops. "It's fun. You'll like it."

Before this week I would have said, "How do you know what I'd like?" My goal to come off bored and older slipped right out from under me. Inside, I felt like I was being pulled onto the sixth-grade dance floor. I wanted to give him my hand and let him pull me up, but I felt too big. Tree limbed. Plain faced. I'd probably look silly on that go-kart, just like I'd look silly matching steps with some boy in the multipurpose room at school.

I glanced down at that sawed-off piece of wood resting on top of a metal frame with skate wheels up front. Tricycle wheels in the back. A rope on one end, a carpet square on the other. I had never seen Hirohito sit on the carpet square. He always rode belly down, arms spread out, and hands gripping the T bar. It was a wonder he wasn't all scarred up.

"Boy, you must be crazy."

"Stop being chicken. You can steer it. Those legs'll reach the turn bar easy. Just hold on to the rope and keep it steady."

Vonetta and Delphine snickered at Hirohito's carefree choice of words.

I couldn't hit him for calling me a long-legged chicken after I had gobbled down his mother's fish and rice. I said, "I am not getting on your street roller. No way."

Instead of saying "Not on your street roller coaster" or "Yeah. No way, Jose," my sisters' voices failed to come to my rescue. Instead, Vonetta and Fern—mostly Vonetta—screamed and danced around us, pleading to take my turn on the go-kart.

Hirohito shook his head, sorely disappointed, like he was Papa. "I didn't think you were scared, Delphine."

"I am not scared of that thing." My voice hit notes it was not known for reaching.

"Then come on."

"No."

"Chicken."

"I am not."

He offered the rope to me and patted the carpet seat. "Just a block. Not even a hill."

I couldn't let him think I was weak and scared. Girl pride and a lower voice said, "I'm not afraid of no hill."

Before I knew it, we had become a merry parade. Me sitting on the go-kart, my feet on the bars, Hirohito behind me pushing, and Vonetta and Fern at the rear, parading up Magnolia Street. What a sight. I sat hunched over, holding on to the rope, my big sneakers on the turn bar. All I could do was wrap the rope tighter around my hands and pray.

How could I find my balance, let alone trust it? Surely balance was needed to ride on that rolling cart of danger. Where was my good common sense? The common sense that Big Ma always pointed out I was born with. I was mad at myself for letting this happen. Letting them push me into riding down some hill on this wooden, bumpy, hot-rod roller. I could fall over on my butt. Scrape every inch of skin on my legs, arms, and hands. I could look a stupid, scraped-up, tangled-up mess, and on top of it all, scream like a fraidycat in front of my sisters.

I hugged the rope. My heart pounded through my ears, down in my toes.

None of that concerned anyone on the parade route.

Hirohito pushed happily. My sisters skipped, clapped, and sang. They might as well have been singing "Crash, Delphine. Crash."

Then Hirohito stopped pushing. Now the tips of my fingers pounded. We were at the top. The very, very top of the hill.

Hirohito looked at me like this was all fine. Not like he was getting me back for being mean to him. My knees would knock if they weren't frozen. I wanted to get up and walk away.

"Don't worry. It's safe," he said. "My dad built it. It's sturdy and has no splinters. He sanded it down for days. Good job, right?"

"Right," I said.

"I helped him." He turned the T part so it swiveled. "Real axle for the turns. It's good for racing. But don't worry," he said again. "You just have to go straight. Keep it steady." He nodded and smiled. "My dad's great."

I doubted he meant to get all girly talking about his father. He caught himself and changed his voice.

"Ready, Delphine?"

I didn't answer.

He said, "Use your sneakers to slow down, then stop. Just drag." Then he lifted my foot and put it in the right position. The position that would turn the heels of my sneakers as doggedy as his. "Remember, you don't have to steer. It's a straight ride down. Just slide your sneaker like this." He moved my foot slightly sideways. It was a wonder he had soles at all.

He told me to hold on tight. Then he ordered Vonetta and Fern to come on as if he had taken my place as the oldest. Part of me didn't like it one bit. The other part didn't have time to think about that.

"Push!"

Vonetta and Fern screamed, *"Yay!"* and I looked up, mad, scared, thrilled.

I felt six hands on my back and the bumpy ground beneath me. With all that rumbling, my head spun with the sheer craziness of it all. Being pushed down the street. My sisters and Hirohito cheering and pushing and letting go and time not ticking but racing away.

It was too late. Too late to jump off while the go-kart rolled, its steel skate wheels hitting every bump and pebble on the sidewalk. I leaned left and right, trying to find my balance. Then forward. Left, right, and forward, my drawn-up knees helping to keep me steady.

There was a curve in the sidewalk. Not exactly straight, like Hirohito told me. To me it was winding, and dangerous like the Chinatown dragon. As the go-kart went faster, I felt the rumbling of the wheels hitting the concrete underneath me. I screamed. So loud I startled myself. I had never heard myself scream. Screamed from the top of my lungs, from the pit of my heart. Screamed like I was snaking and falling. Screamed and hiccupped and laughed like my sisters. Like I was having the time of my life, flying down that glorious hill.

Vonetta, Fern, and Hirohito had run after me, but Hirohito had outrun my sisters and met me at the other end. When we were all together, Hirohito led the parade of him, Vonetta, and Fern, hooting and dancing around me.

The Third Thing

Who would have thought twenty flyers could have brought more than a thousand people to the park? Talk about a grand Negro, well, a grand black spectacle. People simply came, filling up every inch of green in the park. Some even climbed oak trees and perched in branches for a good spot. Everywhere you turned there were college students in T-shirts, signing people up for sickle cell anemia testing and voter registration. Black Panthers from around the country, in sky blue T-shirts with pictures of black panthers on them, stood tall, patrolling the park. Policemen also stood tall, holding on to their wooden clubs.

And yet I wasn't afraid. I was excited.

"You see," Sister Mukumbu said, waving her bangled

arm like a wand over the hundreds of people, maybe a thousand.

I feel ashamed of the pride I take in ironing a crease extrasharp. Ironing a sharp crease is a job well done. Bringing people to this rally was magic that had you soaring above trees. It certainly was worth marching up to the no sayers. In my mind, all these people came to the rally because our summer camp helped to spread the word. The idea of radio announcements, the Black Panther newspaper, and word-of-mouth hadn't entered my mind. If only Cecile could see what we'd done. And Pa and Big Ma.

They put the young people's presentations on first, before all of the speeches and the musicians and the adult poets. Our play was awkward, with Sister Pat following us around with the microphone, but we continued on as if we'd rehearsed it that way. The first time Janice Ankton heard her voice boom out over all those loudspeakers, she jumped back. She soon overcame her amplified voice and proved a bigger ham than Vonetta on her showiest and crowiest days. Janice brandished her silver cap gun at us tired and scared runaway slaves more than Sister Pat's script had called for. All I knew was the crowd liked it, and that was enough for "Harriet Tubman," who proclaimed, "Either you want to be free or you want to be scared slaves!" She was supposed to have said, "I haven't lost a passenger yet." The crowd went crazy, and Janice soaked it up. Eunice kicked her sister the way I sometimes had to put Vonetta in her place. It worked.

Janice stopped waving her silver cap shooter at us and went on with the play as Sister Pat had written it.

After Harriet Tubman freed the slaves, Hirohito and the boys showed off their karate kicks and chops and jujitsu moves. Eunice, Janice, and Beatrice changed into their matching African print head wraps and dresses sewn by their mother.

I was certain Vonetta would be eaten up with jealousy after Janice's loud dramatic performance was soon to be followed by her dancing in that cute matching outfit. Instead, Vonetta had been awfully quiet while we waited for our turn to go onstage. I feared the worst with Vonetta's sunken mood. This had happened just before the Tip Top Tap disaster. A quiet Vonetta was a scared Vonetta. That meant I'd have to dance her part or, in this case, say her part if her eyes bugged out and her mouth didn't open. Then afterward I'd have to "there, there" her for the next two weeks.

"Vonetta, you ready?"

She nodded.

If I didn't make her talk, we were doomed. "What's that, Vonetta?"

Another nod.

Now I was mad. Mad because this was the same Vonetta who had stubbornly wanted to sing "Dry Your Eyes" before all of these people. This was the same Vonetta who had recited "We Real Cool" until it drove Cecile to a cussing fit. This was Vonetta who had said, "We should do this poem."

And as usual, I would have to go out there and finish the mess Vonetta started.

"Vonetta, don't make me kick you."

"Better not," she said. Good. At least her mouth opened and two words came out. "And I'm ready, for your information."

"I'm ready," Fern piped up. "I'm ready like Freddy. I'm ready and steady. I know a boy in my class named Eddie. Eddie Larson, but Larson doesn't go with ready and steady." Then she barked. *"Arf. Arf."*

Vonetta and I looked at each other, then at Fern. Vonetta, said, "Fern, what are you talking about?"

Fern smiled and sang, "I sa-aw something." Then she clapped it out like we were still on the East Bay bus.

The karate boys had run off the platform while the crowd still cheered. I hadn't been paying attention because I was worried about Vonetta. But when Hirohito ran over, I said, "That was really neat."

Sister Pat pushed us to the stage and we marched out before all those people. Vonetta was supposed to introduce us and say the name of our poem and that our mother wrote it. But I could see her eyes growing big and her face ashen. I whispered the two things I knew would get her going. I said, "Hirohito's watching. And Janice hopes you trip."

Vonetta's face ripened to a peach. She grabbed the microphone pole like Diana Ross, stepped out in front of us—her Supremes—then cleared her throat. " 'I Birthed a

195

Black Nation,' by our mother, Nzila, the black poet. All the power to all the people."

The crowd roared and waved their fists. Maybe they carried on because she was a little girl making big sounds. Maybe they cheered for Nzila, who was now a known political prisoner. To Vonetta, they cheered for her, and she was set to show and crow.

Vonetta:
"I birthed a *black* nation.
From my womb *black* creation
spilled forth
to be
stolen
shackled
dispersed."

Me:
"I dispatched *black* warriors
raged against unjust barriers
to find
the *black* and strong had fallen
divided
deceived
overcome."

Fern:

"*Black* oceans separate us

tortured cries

songs

of *black* greatness

Still echo in my canal."

Vonetta, Fern, and me:

"Hear the reverberation

of a stolen *black* nation

forever lost

to foreign shores

where thieves do not atone

and Mother Africa cannot be consoled."

All that was missing was Cecile to see and hear us recite her poem. I'm sure she wouldn't have appreciated Vonetta sprinkling "black" into her poem like pepper, but the crowd loved it, and we went along, following Vonetta's lead, throwing in the word *black* as she had. Following each other was easy. We'd been doing it for as long as we could all talk. Saying Cecile's words, one after another, felt like we were bringing her into our conversation instead of turning our voices on her, like we had.

When we finished, we were supposed to exit the platform—me first, Vonetta second, and Fern last. We'd walked off the stage and over to the wing. That was what I was certain we'd done. Then I turned and saw Fern still standing in the center of the stage. I went to get her, but Sister Pat was already walking out.

Fern wouldn't leave. She said something to Sister Pat, who nodded and adjusted the microphone down to Fern's mouth. Then she left Fern alone onstage.

The crowd quieted and waited, but Fern stood without saying a word. Again I went to get little Fern, but Sister Mukumbu grabbed my shoulder. "Wait, Delphine. Let her."

Sister Mukumbu had no idea how hard it was for me to watch my baby sister stand alone before all of those people. They could laugh at her, shout at her to get off the stage, or boo her into tears. But Fern balled her fists, banged them at her side, and then she spoke.

"My mother calls me Little Girl, but this is a poem by Fern Gaither, not Little Girl. This is a poem for Crazy Kelvin. It's called 'A Pat on the Back for a Good Puppy.'" She cleared her throat.

"Crazy Kelvin says 'Off the pig.'
Crazy Kelvin slaps everyone five.
The policeman pats Crazy Kelvin on the back.
The policeman says, 'Good puppy.'
Crazy Kelvin says, 'Arf. Arf.
Arf, arf, arf, arf.'
Because I saw the policeman pat your back,

Crazy Kelvin.
Surely did."

Two things happened just then. Really, three things.

First, the crowd went wild for Fern Gaither. Janice Ankton folded her arms and told Eunice she didn't want to go onstage and dance after Fern had grabbed up all the applause.

Second, Crazy Kelvin backed away. I think he was searching for the best way to get out of the park, but he was surrounded by Black Panthers. They knew what Fern had said, even though it took Vonetta and me a little longer to really understand what Fern had said and seen. And what it meant. Luckily for Crazy Kelvin, there were enough policemen to step in and get him out of the park.

It's funny about Crazy Kelvin. If he hadn't gone on and on about "racist pigs," Fern would have never asked herself, "What's wrong with this picture?" I'm sure it had more to do with Miss Patty Cake and him telling her who she could love. I'm sure it had more to do with him telling her who she was. Fern had Crazy Kelvin in her sights, and she got him with his own words: "What's wrong with this picture?"

There was a third thing that happened just then, only I didn't know it at the time. Cecile told it to me in a letter a month later. And that thing, the third thing was, a poet had been born. *It wasn't Longfellow,* Cecile had written, *but it was a running start.*

So

Although the rally was still going strong, Vonetta, Fern, and I couldn't get down into the crowd fast enough once we had spotted Cecile. We weren't the hugging type, but we were all happy. We were happy Cecile had been released from jail and happy she was there to see us onstage reciting "I Birthed a Nation." Thanks to Vonetta, now people called Cecile's poem "I Birthed a Black Nation." I had braced myself for her crazy anger at us for disturbing her poem like we disturbed her quiet, but she didn't mention one word about all the "black" we'd thrown into her poem. In fact, Cecile just seemed different after having been locked up. She even limited her disguise to her big shades. She was feeling so good—in a way that I think only I could make out—that she even gave us compliments.

Vonetta got hers at my expense. Cecile said, "See that, Delphine? You need to speak up like Vonetta. Now, that's how you recite a poem." She might as well have said Vonetta was Hollywood's black Shirley Temple. Vonetta lived on Cecile's praise for the rest of the summer and into the next year.

To Fern, Cecile said, "Who said you could write a poem?"

Fern said, "I didn't write it. I said it."

"Surely did," Cecile said, beating her to it; and we all laughed. What Cecile didn't say was Fern's name. Fern didn't seem to notice, but I did.

I waited for Cecile to give me my share of praise. I didn't need it heaped on like my sisters did, but I knew it would be good, because mine would come last. For a change, I planned to roll around in it and grin like a dummy.

But then some of the organizers of the rally swarmed "Sister Nzila" and "Little Nzila." They fussed over Fern, telling her how brave and clever she was. The organizers had also made time for Nzila to speak of her "unjust arrest," but Cecile waved her opportunity away. "Y'all heard my daughters," she said, more tired than proud. "They said it all for me."

Vonetta, Fern, and I hugged Sister Mukumbu and Sister Pat and told them we had a great time at the People's Center summer camp. They praised our work. Praised Fern's bravery. Vonetta's loud, strong voice, and my being a leader and a helper. They told "Sister Nzila" all about us and that they wanted us back next year.

The rest of the rally was all the speeches about Huey Newton and Bobby Hutton. Cecile said she wasn't staying for that, even though she could have been the star of the day. She said, "Y'all can stay and run around with your friends. Tomorrow you'll be on the plane to New York."

Vonetta and Fern ran off with Janice and Beatrice. Eunice and I found a place to sit and share a bag of chips. I told her we would be flying to New York the next day. She asked if we were coming back, and I said I didn't know. I suggested we become pen pals and write each other letters once a month. That sounded okay to her. Neither one of us was really a talker or run-around player. So we just sat there.

Hirohito found us sitting and jumped into a karate pose. "Did you see me?"

"We saw you, Hirohito," Eunice said. "It would have been better if you broke some boards like they do on TV." She demonstrated with a karate chop to a pile of air boards.

He didn't really look at her. He looked at me. "Want a ride on my go-kart?"

I didn't know how to be with Hirohito while Eunice was there. I just said no and looked at my sneakers. I felt my face growing warm. My feet were too big. Too big for a sixth-grade girl.

"Hirohito, you let a girl on your go-kart? Your precious

go-kart?" I couldn't tell if Eunice was teasing him or mad at him.

"Yeah. So."

"You like Delphine."

I hit her on the shoulder like she was Vonetta. She didn't seem to mind. Teasing Hirohito and making me feel silly seemed to provide Eunice with entertainment and satisfaction. She put her hand over her mouth to gasp. "I can't believe you, Delphine. You like Hirohito. You're just as bad as Janice and your sister."

This was the second time Eunice had gotten me, and both times had to do with Hirohito. I never had anyone over me like a sister or brother and didn't know how to answer back. I didn't want to deny it in case he liked me too, but I wasn't about to be the one to say it in words. I hadn't even said it to myself yet.

Eunice wouldn't let up. She was finally enjoying herself. "Hirohito Woods, I can't believe you let a girl ride on your go-kart."

"So."

I smiled without smiling like Cecile does. Besides. He could have said "I don't like her" or "She's too tall" or "She's too plain." He could have said what all the boys in my class said: "I wouldn't like her if she were the last girl on earth." Instead, Hirohito said, "So." Like "Okay." Like it was okay to like Delphine.

I said it too. "So."

Be Eleven

We told Cecile everything. About our excursion to San Francisco, the hippies, Chinatown. Vonetta told how the tall, blond, white people took pictures of her like she was a movie star, which I could see Cecile didn't like one bit. Fern told how she saw Crazy Kelvin with two policemen just before the bus rounded onto the Bay Bridge. She gave us an earful about how Kelvin always said "racist pigs," but he let the policeman pat him on the back like he was the policeman's dog. To that, Cecile said, "If you can see that, then you'll write poems, all right."

We asked her about being arrested and being a political prisoner and a freedom fighter. Cecile made it sound like it was no big deal. "I've been fighting for freedom all my life." But she wasn't talking about protest signs, standing up to the Man, and knowing your rights. She was talking about her life. Just her. Not the people.

Vonetta, wanting more compliments, said, "We put everything back, just the way you like it," talking about Cecile's workplace, the kitchen. I didn't expect gushing, but it would have been nice if she gave us more than the nod.

We packed all of our things except for the clothes we'd wear in the morning. It was hard to believe four weeks had passed by so quickly. When Vonetta and Fern had gone to bed, I went into the kitchen to find Cecile hunched over her printer. Pieces of the machine lay out on the table. She had the screwdriver in her hand, putting it back together herself.

Although I didn't hear the door swing when I pushed it, she had and knew I was there.

"I called your father when I got out," she told me without looking up. "Delphine, why didn't you tell him what happened?"

I stood there, surprised. Shocked. It didn't enter my mind that she would have wanted me to call Papa.

"We thought you were coming right back."

She kept screwing in one of the rollers, still not looking at me directly. "I counted on you to call him. Tell him what happened. I at least thought you'd figure that out. You're the oldest, Delphine. The smart one."

She had just told me I was smart and a disappointment, reminding me she hadn't said one nice thing to me. Not one.

"Papa would have made us come back to Brooklyn. He would have been mad because I didn't do what he said: look after Vonetta and Fern. And then Big Ma wouldn't let a day pass without telling me for the rest of my life how you aren't nothing but—"

"Delphine. You let seven days pass without calling your father. Seven days. That would have been looking out for Vonetta and Afua. You shouldn't have taken this all on yourself. You didn't have nothing to do with the police arresting me. I didn't have nothing to do with the police arresting me. They came. They arrested me along with the two Panthers they really wanted. And Louis's mother is going to say whatever she's going to say. That's just how it is. All you had to do was call your father. That was all."

My eyes stung. I was spilling-over mad. I couldn't stop what I had to say, even if she stood over me and became my crazy mother mountain and knocked me down. I was spilling over.

"I'm only eleven years old, and I do everything. I have to because *you're* not there to do it. I'm only eleven years old, but I do the best I can. I don't just *up and leave.*"

I was still on two feet. There was no sting on my jaw. My backside had not been touched. But I was ready for it. I closed my eyes, because I figured the slap wouldn't sting as much when it did come.

Instead I heard metal on metal. I opened my eyes. The sound I heard was the screwdriver missing the groove, hitting the printer's metal innards. She laid the screwdriver on the table.

I had nowhere to go, but I wanted to disappear.

Finally, she nodded to the floor and said, "Sit."

I did what she told me. There was a lot of silence, but then she spoke.

"It was just me and my mother until I was eleven."

I wasn't used to having her attention. Having her look at me and talk. All the while she spoke, she didn't lift her eyes from me.

"A car hit her and she was gone. That was it. My aunt took me in to clean her house. Watch her kids. I slept on a blanket on the floor in the kids' room for five years. I was sixteen when she announced she was getting married. She said it wasn't good for a big gal like me to be in her house, seeing as she had a husband. She said in the long run she was doing me a favor. Then my mother's sister made me a sandwich I couldn't eat, gave me twenty dollars, and put me out.

"I slept in subways at night. During the daytime I read Homer and Langston Hughes in libraries. I tried to hide in the stacks, but they always found me and shooed me out. When I didn't have fifteen cents for the subway, I slept on park benches. Wherever I could hide myself.

"Delphine, it's a hard thing to sleep on the streets. A hard thing for a grown man. A harder thing for a teenage girl, no matter how big and tall she is. At night I talked to myself to stay awake. I said the poems of Homer and Langston Hughes. I liked the words. They comforted me. Their rhymes. Their beats. They made a place for me. They kept me strong.

"But I was always hungry, and I had gotten sick. Your father found me on a park bench. He and his brother had a nice apartment on Herkimer Street. He fed me. Gave me a bed to sleep on. I hadn't slept on a bed since I was eleven years old and my mother was alive.

"Louis never bothered me. Didn't ask me to do much but cook. Sweep. Wash his clothes." She paused. "I had you the next year. Six years from where you are now. I had Vonetta next. Both times his mother came up from Alabama and delivered you and Vonetta in that apartment. She and I couldn't get along, so she always went back south.

"Then I had the last one. That little one wanted out bad enough to come when she wanted to come. Early and fast. She was born on a Friday. All I could do was lie on the kitchen floor and let her come."

She stopped for a minute and said, "You were there when she came."

"I was?"

"I was down on the floor. You stroked my hair like I was

a doll, but you didn't have any dolls. No toys. You said, 'Don't cry, Mama. Don't cry.' I think that's the first time I heard you really speak. But when she came out of me, you didn't say a word. You took the dish towel hanging off the icebox handle and wiped off your sister."

I could hardly breathe.

"Then Darnell walked in from school. He did everything else needed to be done."

Why couldn't I remember seeing Fern being born? Telling my mother not to cry. Wiping Fern off with the dish towel. Where were those flashes of memory?

"Your life seems hard, Delphine, but it is good. It's better than what I could have given you."

Here was my mother telling me her life. Who she was. How she came to be Cecile. Answering questions I'd stored in my head from the time I realized she would not come back. Here she was telling me more than I could remember, understand, picture. Maybe I was too young to really take hold of it all, but for what seemed like the first time ever all I could think about was my own self. What I lost. What I missed. That no one said, "Good, Delphine." No one ever said thank-you. Even after her telling me all of this, I was still mad. Maybe I'd been mad all along but didn't have time to just be it. Mad.

"Is it true what Big Ma says? That you left because you couldn't name Fern?"

I took her silence as a yes. For a while she said nothing,

so I guessed she was done talking. I started to get up.

Then she said, "I could've taken you with me and left the other two. You have my mother's face. You didn't cry. You didn't want much. You didn't talk, but you understood. But I didn't have a penny in my pocket. I just knew I had to go. So I gave Vonetta a cookie. That was all she wanted anyway. I gave the baby milk and I . . ."

The picture flashed before me as it had many, many times.

". . . put the doll baby in with Afua. The doll I asked Darnell to go to the store and get. I told you to be good and wait for Papa. Then I left."

She told me everything I wanted to know and too much. It was too much. I'd have to take it out one piece at a time to look at it.

She said, "Did I leave because of a name? You'd have to be grown first before I explained. If I told you now, it would just be words." She picked up her screwdriver and went back to working on her printer. "Be eleven, Delphine. Be eleven while you can."

That was it.

In the middle of the night I woke up.

Afua?

Afua

"Delphine, Vonetta, and Fern! Get up outta that bed. Come on, y'all. It's time to go."

No one wanted to get out of bed. No one wanted to go. But Cecile stood in the doorway and called us one more time.

Fern was the first to spring up. "Hey. That's my name. Our mother said my name!"

Cecile rolled her eyes and left the room.

Fern was a regular jumping bean. "She said my name! She said my name!"

Vonetta couldn't take another excited minute of Fern jumping on the upper mattress. "Big deal. She said my name too."

"Big deal to me," Fern said. "She always says Delphine. She always says Vonetta. Today she said Fern, Fern, Fern." She jumped in between each "Fern." "Fern. Not Little Girl."

Vonetta flung her pillow at Fern, but Fern wouldn't be quieted.

I said, "That's not your real name. The one she gave you."

"It is too."

"Is not."

We kept it up, Vonetta and I on the same side for a change. "Is too."

Then I broke it by saying, "Your name is Afua."

I wasn't known for joking. That sobered them as much as Fern's name, which they both mouthed. A-FOO-A.

"Take that back, Delphine," Fern said. "My name's not Afua. It's Fern."

Vonetta pointed at her. "Ah-hah! Afoowah. Phooey. Chop Suey. Little Phooey. All over my shoo-ie."

Fern turned red. This was the part where I was supposed to shut Vonetta up and take Fern's side. Instead I said, "Get used to it. Your name is Afua, as in Delphine, Vonetta, and Afua."

Fern balled her fingers into a fist and punched me in the stomach. Her hand was so little. I didn't say "Ow!" to give her the satisfaction of knowing she caused me pain. I just said, "Go brush your teeth, Afua."

Later, Cecile said, "Why'd you tell her that? If I wanted her to know her name, I would have told her."

I couldn't tell if Cecile was really annoyed or if she was just fussing. I decided she was fussing and that I couldn't go through my life afraid of what my mother might do next. I shrugged and ate my cereal.

Delphine, Vonetta, Afua, Nzila. Some names made up. Some not. Did it matter what they really meant, or where Cecile got them from, as long as she gave them to us and to herself?

We spent the bus ride and the two-dollar taxi ride to the airport making fun of Afua. Once Cecile said "Cut it out," that was the end of us teasing Fern outright. Still, Vonetta and my constant smirks erupted into snickers. Fern stayed mad.

When we got to the airport, Cecile called Papa collect. She turned her back to us and spoke to Pa for more than fifteen minutes. Big Ma wouldn't be happy about the cost of the collect call, but I doubted Papa minded.

While we waited for Cecile to finish speaking with Pa, a white man came by and said how cute my sisters and I were in our matching outfits. He still had film left over from his sightseeing trip and wanted to use the last of it to take a picture of us. "Pretty girls, smile pretty!" he said. I could tell he was a nice man, but Cecile put a stop to it while Vonetta adjusted her hair band, already posing for the cover of *Jet*.

Cecile stood in front of us and said, "They're not monkeys on display." The nice man tried to apologize, but Cecile wouldn't hear it. "How'd you like it if some strange man came snapping pictures of your daughters?" I felt bad for him, but I knew Cecile had to step in. Any mother would have at least done that.

We sat in comfy waiting-room seats without talking for almost half an hour. The hands on the big clock moved slowly. Fern nodded merrily like she was answering herself or singing. Kind of like Cecile tapping out beats with her pencil. Vonetta fiddled with her hair band or twirled her longest braid around her finger. I followed the janitor pushing his dry mop along the floor as people carrying travel bags danced around him or found seats. I stopped glancing up at the big clock or down at my Timex. I didn't have to. The queasiness churning inside told me it was time to go. And then the boarding announcement was made over the loudspeaker.

She said, "Go on," and we went.

I expected Cecile to walk away. To cut through the terminal in man-sized strides as soon as we got up and stood on line. When I turned to see if she had gone, she was standing only a few feet away, looking straight at me. It was a strange, wonderful feeling. To discover eyes upon you when you expected no one to notice you at all. I smiled a little and faced front to find something to do with myself.

Vonetta and Fern both held on to their own ticket. I

reached to take Fern's ticket, afraid she'd crush it the way she was holding it. She felt me reaching and pulled her hand away. We moved closer to the front of the line near the ticket taker. Fern balled both hands, banging her fists at her sides, her ticket now completely crumpled.

Maybe she was afraid of the airplane ride and getting knocked around by those clouds. Maybe she didn't know what to do with her hands without Miss Patty Cake. Or she could have still been mad about all that Afua teasing. My first move was to comfort her. I went to reach out to Fern, but she bolted from the line, ran, and jumped on top of Cecile. Vonetta and I didn't hesitate. We broke off from the line and ran over to hug our mother and let her hug us.

How do you fly three thousand miles to meet the mother you hadn't seen since you needed her milk, needed to be picked up, or were four going on five, and not throw your arms around her, whether she wanted you to or not? Neither Vonetta, Fern, nor I could answer that one. We weren't about to leave Oakland without getting what we'd come for. It only took Fern to know we needed a hug from our mother.

Acknowledgments

There are so many women and girls in this story. Women I've known. Poets I grew up reading. Girlhood friends. Through the writing, the people who kept me inspired were my hurricane of a mother, Miss Essie Mae Coston Williams, my own "Delphine"—Rosalind Williams Rogers, Rashamella Cumbo, Debra Bonner, Ruby Whitaker, and so many more. Among the poets I thought of during the writing were Nikki Giovanni, Gwendolyn Brooks, Lucille Clifton, Sonia Sanchez, and Kattie Miles Cumbo. And where would this work be without my sister, champion, and editor: Rosemary Brosnan?

I could not have written this work of fiction without having read books, articles, and interviews that cover this period. I specifically could not have felt the climate of the times from Black Panther accounts and perspectives without David Hilliard's *The Black Panther Intercommunal News Service.*

I wanted to write this story for those children who witnessed and were part of necessary change. Yes. There were children.

ONE CRAZY SUMMER

An Excerpt from Rita Williams-Garcia's Acceptance
Speech for the Coretta Scott King Author Award for
One Crazy Summer

A Deleted Chapter from the Novel

Extras and Activities

An Excerpt from Rita Williams-Garcia's Acceptance Speech for the Coretta Scott King Author Award for *One Crazy Summer*

Throughout my work, I've invited my mostly teen readers to ponder my offerings and form their own opinions. In my seventh novel I wanted to do something different. I wanted to share an era in which I had enjoyed my childhood—the late 1960s. Much to my delight and amusement, this is a historical period for eleven-year-olds today.

Let me backtrack for a minute and repeat: "I had enjoyed my childhood." In spite of the necessary upheaval going on in the country and the world, in spite of having to pull up stakes and move because my father was in the army, in spite of being reminded that tomorrow was not promised, I enjoyed my childhood. My siblings and I indulged in now-vanishing pastimes. We played hard. Read books. Colored with crayons. Rode bikes. Spoke as children spoke. Dreamed our childish dreams. If our parents did anything for us at all, they gave us a place to be children and kept the adult world in its place—as best as they could. But curious eyes and ears always latch onto something.

While my father was in Vietnam, my mother did volunteer work with an antipoverty program. Decades later she would say on video that she was a member of the Black Panther Party, although I knew Miss Essie was playing to the camera. But as quiet as history tends to keep certain details, the Black Panther Party for Self-Defense was founded by activists within an antipoverty program, so I can't entirely discount Miss Essie. We did, however, have relatives who were members of or involved with the Black Panthers and the Black Liberation Army. When I was around ten or eleven, my ears caught hold of whispering about a cousin I never knew I had: a college student who had hijacked a plane to Algeria. There was more talk about other family members that my siblings and I weren't privy to.

After my father's discharge from service, our family returned to St. Albans, New York, and found a strong Black Panther presence in the neighborhood. It was a presence that contradicted the images in the news. I cannot tell you that those images were false; they just weren't what I saw as a child. In my neighborhood I observed the expression of Black Panther ideology in poetry, in music, and on posters. There were free clinics and sickle-cell anemia testing. Free breakfast programs. Clothing and shoe giveaways. There were children's programs, although I never attended any. As an older teen, I followed the imprisonments of Angela Davis and Assata Shakur, known then as JoAnne Chesimard. I learned that Assata Shakur, like Black Panther activist Afeni Shakur, had been pregnant while incarcerated. I wondered about the children of Black Panther Party members.

When I sat down to write *One Crazy Summer*, I chose children and childhood as my entrée into the Black Power Movement. Children were being born into the revolution. Children were ever present and at the heart of the ideals of change and revolution. They were served by the Black Panther Party in community programs and attended Black Panther–run schools, such as the Oakland Community School. They learned to be intellectually curious and aware, and to serve within their communities. In many cases, children were sheltered in safe houses because they were children of the revolution.

I had only to look at the picture of the young sons of former Black Panther Party Chief of Staff David Hilliard to put things into childlike perspective. Even children of the revolution yearn for their mothers and fathers. The late rapper and poet Tupac Shakur, son of Afeni Shakur, expressed his own ambivalence toward his mother's devotion to "the cause," although this didn't hinder his political awareness. I had to remember to take the story to a personal level and to not allow myself to get carried away with my own zeal. To remember that children of revolution, children of activism, know what it is to live with sacrifice and a child's heartbreak. I only hoped that, like last year's Coretta Scott King honorees, I'd give light and life to an overlooked, underappreciated, and often misrepresented period in our nation's history. And to do that, I followed as Delphine, Vonetta, Fern, and Hirohito lead me in all the right ways.

A Deleted Chapter from the Novel

Maxie's Printing and Supplies

"Delphine."

I heard her and went. Vonetta and Fern followed even though they weren't called.

"Get your sneakers on and go to Acme Stationers and get me some paper. One ream, fifty-pound velum. It's on the paper." She shoved the paper and a five-dollar bill in my hand. "Just give the man this."

I didn't know what she was telling me. Just paper at the stationery store. As long as the name was on the slip of paper I didn't have to ask questions, and I knew that's what she wanted. For me to just do what she said and not ask any questions.

"Take the same bus we came here on. Catch it around the corner. It's a few stores down from Maxie's Printing and Supplies but don't go in Maxie's. Stay away from Maxie's. Y'hear?"

Vonetta and Fern chirped, "We wanna go."

Cecile dug into her man's pants pockets and emptied some change in our hands. She said to me, "If you were grown, they'd ride for free. But you gotta pay for them. Go on."

Eleven going on twelve ain't hardly grown, but sometimes I'm tired like a grown woman. At the same time I have energy to do everything that needs to get done. And I wonder if I would be different if Cecile never left. If I wouldn't be watching my sisters or ironing their clothes or straightening their hair or giving them Vicks VapoRub if Cecile never left.

We walked to the bus stop. We needed only a dime each, but Cecile dumped too much change in Vonetta's and Fern's hands. I have pockets and say, "Hand it over."

"No," they both said.

"Where's your pockets, then?" I ask because neither of their shorts have pockets. Only mine do.

Vonetta said, "I don't need pockets."

"Me neither."

I tap my foot and plant my hands on my hips. Even though I'm not grown I can fake it. "Don't come crying to me when it falls out of your hands."

Fern was the first to hand over her change. Her hands

were too small. She had already grown tired of shifting the coins from hand to hand. Finally Vonetta gave in.

"But we want candy," she said.

"Jolly Ranchers."

"Pixy Stix."

"Wax lips."

"And Bit-O-Honeys."

And they went on naming all the penny candies when we got on the bus. I think they liked naming the candies more than they wanted to eat them.

We watched boys on skateboards ride down the hill and disappear around the wide curve. Vonetta and Fern gasped and cheered at what looked like fun to them, but to me looked like scraped knees, twisted ankles, and Big Ma scolding, "Why'd you let them out of your sight?" There was nothing fun about flying down and around a hill and a winding curve on a rolling plank of wood. I doubt Cecile kept iodine and Band-Aids in the medicine cabinet. I doubt Cecile would do more than grunt and say, "If you fall, you fall," or some kind of *makes no difference to me* remark.

Fun to Vonetta and Fern usually meant trouble for me. They could watch the skateboarders all they wanted from our seats on the bus. There was no way I was letting them ride a skateboard. Or a go-kart. If Hirohito Woods's mother let him ride down hills in that shake-rattle-and-roll cart, those were his scraped knees and hers to clean. And why was I thinking about Hirohito Woods anyway? What did he have to do with anything?

When we got to Acme Stationers I gave the man the slip of paper. "One ream" was what I remembered, but it was safer to hand the man the slip of paper than come back with the wrong thing.

He had the fifty-pound paper, which didn't feel like fifty pounds. Fern weighed forty-eight pounds. I knew what that felt like. All the same, the paper was heavy. I took it and we left.

An old man with a mustache smoked a cigar and swept the sidewalk outside of Maxie's Printing and Supplies. Usually grown-ups look at Fern and say how cute she is. They might look at Vonetta because she tries so hard to be seen. But no one looks at me. The old man sweeping did. In fact, he came up to me, stared in my face, nodded hard and angry, and dropped the cigar from his mouth.

"Thief!"

I backed away from this mustachioed man and his cigar breath. My sisters clung to me. He was short for a man, heavy and old.

"Thief!"

"I'm no thief!" I said.

"Me neither."

"Me either."

That didn't stop him. "Thief!" he said. "I know stealing thieves when I see them." His face grew red.

A younger woman came outside from the shop. She told him, "Maxie, calm down. Maxie, don't."

We walked away and looked for the bus stop. We didn't even bother to go inside the candy store.

I was glad to be back and gave Cecile her change and her fifty-pound paper. But Vonetta spilled the beans.

"You shoulda seen it. There was a man sweeping the street. He took one look at Delphine and said, 'Thief!'"

Cecile was not entertained, as Vonetta hoped she would be. Cecile was angry. Not at Vonetta or Maxie, but at me. "Don't you listen? I told you not to go by Maxie's."

"It was two stores away from the stationery store."

"You should have walked around."

Walked around? Who thinks like that? A secret-agent mother. Or maybe like Maxie said. A thief.

Extras and Activities

1. Nineteen sixty-eight was a revolutionary time for politics and music. In her PBS interview, former Black Panther Kathleen Cleaver said, "We were doing to politics what Jimi Hendrix was doing to music. We were changing the volume, changing the rhythm."

   - Working in groups or independently, put together a playlist of ten songs that reflect the 1960s and scenes from *One Crazy Summer*.
   - Choose a song from your list and present a "song talk" to your audience. Play at least one minute of the song and discuss the meaning of the lyrics and how the song relates to the 1960s or *One Crazy Summer*.

2. Cecile/Nzila wrote poems during the time women writers such as Nikki Giovanni, Sonja Sanchez, and Lucille Clifton wrote poetry.

   - Adopt a poet of the 1960s and study one of his or her poems.
   - Hold a poetry recital.
   - Write your own poems.
   - With your parents' permission, videotape yourself as the characters and perform "Moveable Type," "A Good Dog," or "I Birthed a Black Nation." Post on YouTube, and include *One Crazy Summer* in your site title.

3. The Black Panther Party was originally founded in 1966 as an organization of self-defense and community

activism, although people within and outside of the black community didn't necessarily agree with their message and methods.

- Visit the Black Panther website at www.blackpanther. org/TenPoint.htm and read the Black Panther's Ten Point Program, a document that outlines their basic wants.
- Take each point (for example, "WE WANT FULL EMPLOYMENT FOR OUR PEOPLE") and discuss— Agree or disagree. Do you agree or disagree up to a point?

4. The 1960s was a decade of protest and change. Each protest had its own rallying message. Supporters carried signs and wore buttons. Some protest messages used words, some messages included a logo, and others included both words and a logo.

- Find a cause that you believe in.
- Write a short memorable message for your cause.
- Optional: Design a logo for your cause.
- Create a protest sign, button, or T-shirt using your protest message and logo.

5. Time lines are a good way to study a period of time. Why not take a glance at the 1960s, from the beginning to the end of the decade?

- Choose a topic (i.e. fashion, politics, news headlines, inventions, music, popular dances, space exploration).
- Using a large sheet or roll of paper and a ruler, draw a time line, marking each year from 1960 to

1970. Each "year point" should be equidistant to the next year point. (For example, if your time line is ten inches long, each year point should be one inch long.) Depending on the size of your paper, you can make your year point as close together or as far apart as you like.

- Use both graphics and text to describe the events you wish to include along the points of your time line.

6. Delphine, Vonetta, and Fern go on an excursion to San Francisco. Prior to going, Delphine gets travel and sightseeing information from the library. Plan your own excursion.

- Choose a city or country that you'd like to visit.
- Plan a trip by gathering information about the best way to travel, sights to see, food that is special to the place, and souvenirs that reflect the city or country you chose.
- Create a budget for all of your travel, sightseeing, and souvenir needs.
- Design a postcard that represents your adventure.

"Regimented, responsible, strong-willed Delphine narrates in an unforgettable voice, but each of the sisters emerges as a distinct, memorable character, whose hard-won, tenuous connections with their mother build to an aching, triumphant conclusion."

—ALA *Booklist* (starred review)

"Delphine is the pitch-perfect older sister, wise beyond her years, an expert at handling her siblings. While the girls are caught up in the difficulties of adults, their resilience is celebrated and energetically told with writing that snaps off the page."

—*Kirkus Reviews* (starred review)

"Emotionally challenging and beautifully written, this book immerses readers in a time and place and raises difficult questions of cultural and ethnic identity and personal responsibility. With memorable characters (all three girls have engaging, strong voices) and a powerful story, this is a book well worth reading and rereading."

—*School Library Journal* (starred review)

"Delphine's growing awareness of injustice on a personal and universal level is smoothly woven into the story in poetic language that will stimulate and move readers."

—*Publishers Weekly*